Murder Most Picante

A DragonEye, PI story

Karina Fabian

Laser Cow Press

ROCKLEDGE, FL

Laser Cow Press
Rockledge, FL
https://fabianspace.com

Publisher's Note: This is a work of fiction. Names, characters, places, and incidents are a product of the author's imagination. Locales and public names are sometimes used for atmospheric purposes. Any resemblance to actual people, living or dead, or to businesses, companies, events, institutions, or locales is completely coincidental.

Cover art by Dawn Grimes
DragonEye Logo by Len Fabian

Murder Most Picante/Karina Fabian -- 1st ed.
ISBN 978-1-7334471-3-3

Dedication

To all the Vern fans who patiently waited for the next novel. Vern says that no amount of clapping your hands and saying you believe keeps a fairy from dying, but we know that your love for Vern kept him alive.

She has a point, but don't rub it in.

Contents

Chapter One: Dragon vs. Crazy Cat Lady 3
Chapter Two: Demons and Damsels................ 16
Chapter Three: Fire and I.C.E. 36
Chapter Four: Dragon Gets a Job..................... 54
Chapter Five: LARPing and Harping 70
Chapter Six: No Good Deed............................. 84
Chapter Seven: Parish Grounded................... 100
Chapter Eight: Visit to a Safe Space............... 114
Chapter Nine: Dragon Plays D&D 127
Chapter Ten: Lawyer Up 146
Chapter Eleven: Commandos, Cars, and the Crazy Cat Lady.. 162
Chapter Twelve: Dragon Goes Home 186
Chapter Thirteen: Ring Around the Damsel.... 207
Chapter Fourteen: Bad Chemistry, Worse Magic 226
Chapter Fifteen: Confessions and Karma 247
Chapter Sixteen: Crazy Cat Lady Comes Through 258
Acknowledgements....................................... 281
Thanks for Reading 283

Chapter One: Dragon vs. Crazy Cat Lady

Humans were made in God's image.

Dragons, on the other hand... We came from God's Imagining.

We are the eighth day creation, limited in number but unending in days, and God gifted us to the Faerie world so no one would forget His great power. We commanded the respect of empyrie from Ur-kuk, the Harbinger of Hiccups, to Zeus himself. Elves described our virtues in poetry that took days to recite. Dwarves honored us by creating expansive cave lairs in their mines just in case a dragon decided to visit. And humans? Well, Image often clashed with Imagination. Nonetheless, even humans acknowledged our majesty.

I am a dragon, and once I ranked among the greatest of my kind.

I'm not telling you this to brag. I'm telling you this so you can appreciate the level of restraint I practiced while a five-foot octogenarian poked her walker at my nose and screamed at me in Spanish about her cat.

Señora Dona Elena Costa was on the downhill slide of her 80s: crippled, half-blind, and possessing a vocabulary that would have made Coronado's men blush. Trust me. I sailed with the Conquistadors. I know.

Señora Costa lived across the street from Little Flower Parish in Los Lagos, Colorado, where I'd taken up residence after crossing from the Faerie world to the Mundane. Señora Costa had somewhere between 17 and 40 cats, and even though the number changed daily and she was half blind, she possessed the uncanny ability to know when one went missing. The woman knew her cats like I knew my treasure, and I respected her for it.

Unfortunately, cats, unlike gold, jewels, and rare artifacts, tend to wander and get lost. Regardless of whether the missing feline had an unlucky encounter with a car or a lucky meeting with a starry-eyed six-year-old with accommodating parents, whenever one went missing, Señora Costa suspected a crime. Lately, that meant the resident dragon must have done it.

This is your fault, George, I thought at the Faerie saint. I imagined him snickering in reply. He had that kind of humor. I could almost hear him quoting Paul's lament about a thorn in his flesh.

My current thorn had exhausted her litany of accusations and derisive commentary. As she paused to catch her breath, I jumped in.

"Señora, I did not eat your Sasha. I haven't eaten any of your cats."

Getting Crazy Cat Lady to believe me was about as likely as Sasha showing up and curling herself around my legs, but I had to try. After all, God had given me a Calling to emigrate to the Mundane, and if I was ever going to figure out what He wanted me to do here, I had to get the Mundanes thinking of me as a person and not a talking animal.

Bishop Aiden's words echoed in my mind's ear: "Mundanes are a judgmental and paranoid lot, Vern. You must be patient with them. Remember, you aren't there for yourself, so much as for all of Faerie. You can thank Saint George for that."

I often do. With a lot of snark and venom.

Señora Costa's eyes narrowed behind her coke-bottle glasses, and she took several deep breaths to prepare herself for her next onslaught. This was probably the most excitement she got anymore, and she was certainly making the most of it.

"Listen, lady," I started in Spanish. "Let me explain a little about the dietary preferences of dragons."

"I don't want to hear your lies!" She slammed her walker down with a thud that knocked off one of its tennis ball feet.

So, I'm a liar now, too? I flexed my claws. "See any blood? No? Look closer. You won't find any. Want to check my teeth for fur, too?"

Would you believe the feisty old biddy said yes?

I opened my jaws good and wide. She shoved her walker aside, braced her hands on my chin and snout, and stuck her head into my mouth calling, "*Sasha, gatita! Ven! Michimichimichi...*"

That's when Father Rich and Sister Bernadette walked in on us.

Sister Bernadette screamed and ran for the first weapon she could find—a leaf rake. She started to swing at my nose, a singularly bad idea considering I had an octogenarian's head between my teeth. I yanked my head back while swinging my tail to block her shot.

Sister Bernadette fell against a workbench, bounced, and came back ready to swing again. Señora Costa toppled and fell hard on her rump. She yelped out a new swear word. And here I thought she'd run out.

Me, I banged my head against the garage door motor and let out a swear word of my own. Of course, to human ears, it sounded like the wild roar of a feral beast. Which is why Sister Bernadette smacked me.

I yanked the rake out of her hands. "Seriously, Sister? Next time, get a pitchfork and do it right."

Señora Costa, not one to be out of the center of attention, started bawling that she just wanted to find her poor, sweet Sasha.

"Which you won't find in my mouth," I sniped back, "or down my throat, in my stomach, or out my–"

"Sister Bernadette!" Father Rich hollered over my words as he pulled the rake from my grasp, "Why don't you take Dona Elena inside for some tea?"

Convinced I was all bark and no bite, at least for the moment, Ninja Nun relaxed from her defensive posture and helped Señora Costa with her walker. We waited in silence as Sister Bernadette supported her elderly charge, who shuffled and blubbered her way to the steps leading into the rectory. At the top of the short flight of stairs, she stopped to give me the stink eye before resuming her sniffling as she walked through the door.

When the latch clicked, Father let out a sigh. "Vern, have a seat."

I didn't know what he expected me to do, since my rump was already on the ground, but I relaxed my posture and settled in like one of Isis's cats. Meanwhile, he set the rake aside and pulled over a folding chair from where it leaned against a workbench. Once he settled himself, I could see from his posture what was coming. This wasn't the first time I'd been "lovingly counseled" by a man of the cloth.

"You've been here in the Mundane...two months now?"

I nodded. "One month in the military camp at the Gap while they tried to determine if I was a threat or not, and three weeks here with you." I probably should have thanked him, but Señora Gataloca's curlers had scratched the roof of my mouth. I wasn't feeling especially grateful for the new neighbors.

Father nodded encouragingly, but when I didn't add anything, he asked, "So? What are you doing here?"

It was a good question, for which I had no good answer. It was not my idea, after all.

When the combination magic spell and nuclear accident created the portal between our dimensions, I was "enjoying" a quiet, Church-ordered respite with the Silent Brothers, where my biggest concerns were whether I'd have to pull the plow again and where I'd find a decent conversation. I didn't think about the incident other than to call Duke Galen a fool for hiring cheap mages and laugh at the ridiculous name given to something as amazing as a stable interdimensional portal. They called it "the Gap."

But neither it nor the name were any of my business...at least until Brother Matthias woke from a vision and said I was to cross the Gap into the Mundane.

I laughed at him and went to the South Field for a nap.

Then Bishop Aiden came to me. He'd apparently had the same vision.

I made a promise to take it under advisement and rolled over to resume my snooze. I may have missed the Great Hibernation that kept all my fellow dragons safe and hidden from everyone (including me), but I could sleep for days when I got the notion.

Then St. George came to me in a vision of my own.

George and I have a history. The first time we met, he'd demanded I place myself under his command. I countered with an invitation to join me for lunch—as the main course. That started an epic battle that ended with me losing my size, my magic, my skills, my strength, my memories...and then he pressed me into serving sapients under the direction of the Faerie Catholic Church as the way to regain all that made me dragon. I've been at it over eight centuries, and I'm still undersized, underpowered, and without my fire.

When he appeared and told me to cross the Gap, I knew better than to argue, especially since he had the same determined, divinely inspired twinkle in his eye.

That was seven weeks ago. I wish now I'd paused at least long enough to ask him why.

My introspection was lost on Father. "Well?" he demanded impatiently.

"I don't know. And even if I did, I don't think I'll accomplish anything here, anyhow. Not with the way you Mundanes have reacted. This is the third time this week alone that Señora Gataloca has accused me of snatching kittens."

"Well, we can't keep going like this. Every day, I'm fielding complaints. The parish council is still up in arms about my opening our home to you."

"You gave me the garage."

"Where else are you going to fit? You're almost the size of a horse!"

I snorted. Almost the size of a horse. Once upon a time, I could have snatched up a horse in my claws and carried it into the clouds without breaking a sweat, as the humans say. Now, if I was almost the size of a horse, it was more like a pony.

"I didn't ask for this," I told Father. "I wanted to find a nice cave in the mountains and set up there. But something called the EPA forbad it. Said I was a danger to the environment. How can

I be a danger to the environment? It's not like I can set fire to anything."

Father shrugged. "Because you're not native to the area. It's like when we introduced rabbits to Australia..."

I'd heard this one before. "Rabbits?" I snapped. "How can you compare me to a rabbit? I am a *sapient* creature. Besides, there's only one of me, and dragons don't breed, like rabbits or otherwise."

Father had an argument on his tongue, but at my statement, he paused and blinked. "You don't?"

I looked at him in askance. Maybe I should write a pamphlet or something. *The Care and Feeding of God's Most Awesome Creation.* "God created us as the ultimate, glorious, apex predator. I know I don't look like much now, but pre-George, I was phenomenal. All my kind were. We are nearly unstoppable and immortal. Do you really think God didn't have the foresight to limit our numbers?

"My kind was meant to be regarded with awe. We are the living embodiment of the unfathomable, amazing imagination of our Creator. In

Faerie, they understood that. Even in my diminished state, I received some respect due my kind. Here, you humans compare me to large rodents. Don't think I haven't heard Mrs. Davis accusing me of trampling her flower garden. And her neighbor, Sir Grumpy of the Black Thumb, who thinks I'm using his vegetable garden as my toilet. He should be so lucky."

"Vern, I know. And I've defended you to the parishioners. But you have to think about it from our perspective. We have never seen an actual dragon before. You are completely new to us. How would we know about your former grandeur, much less dragon toilet habits?"

Then, he frowned. "Just where are you 'going,' anyway?"

Three weeks I've been here, and now he asks? "You haven't noticed how well the roses are growing?"

"You're going in the prayer garden?" He paused to cross his forehead, something he did when asking for patience, then clenched his hand into a fist. He pointed it toward me as if to show how much effort he was making. "We'll hold that conversation for later. Listen, I understand you were sent here. Bishop Aiden told me about the visions. You must have a purpose, but I don't think your Calling is to sit in my garage, eating, watching TV, and complaining about the neighbors! You need to find something constructive to do."

"Like what? Get a job?"

"It would be a start."

My mouth fell open wide enough for a kitten to jump in. I let a Mundane poke me with her walker, swear at me, and stick her head in my mouth without even drooling, and the conclusion he draws is I need a job?

"Would you like to drive me over to wherever Mundanes go to get hired? Wisdom of the Ages, Experience of Eternity, but you know the first thing they will probably ask is if I'm housebroken!"

Now Father raised his voice, "All right then, what do you want to do?"

I laughed. "Oh, no! The last time I tried to do what I wanted to do in this world, people shot at me and then I was shoved into the Sheriff's car and brought here. And speaking of..."

I jerked my head to indicate Sheriff Bert Wheeler standing behind Father in the open garage doorway.

“Sounds like a pretty heated argument. Am I interrupting?” Bert asked in his friendly but authoritative way. You know, the way that says, "I don't really care if I’m interrupting because if things get more heated, people might end up in cuffs." I think all law enforcement officers practice that tone.

“Just trying to work some things out,” Father said.

“Father was giving me vocational counseling,” I added and ignored the priest’s glare.

“Riiight,” Bert said, then got to business. “I don't know what that was about, but you two can work it out later. Father, I wondered if you had some time to come with me to McTaggert Farms. There's been a death among the farmhands."

Father gave a start and quickly rose from the chair and replaced it in its corner. "Absolutely. Is there family to comfort?"

Bert shrugged. "From what Juarez said, people are kind of relieved he's dead. Problem is how he died. The migrants think a demon did it."

Chapter Two: Demons and Damsels

I expected Father Rich to run for his exorcism kit or whatever Mundane priests used for spiritual battle. Instead, he raised a brow at Bert. "A demon? Really?"

Bert shrugged. "Juarez's out there talking to them now. They are convinced a demon has taken over the fields. They think the whole area's possessed. I wouldn't be bothering you otherwise. Couldn't you just come with me, splash some water, say some prayers?"

"Splash some water?" I squawked. I know not all humans in this world are Catholic, but *splash some water*? Dragons have dealt with demons since the beginning of time. It wasn't easy when I was at my full strength, magic, and glory. After my last battle, I spent nearly a century in a monastery recovering from the physical and spiritual damage, not to mention the indigestion.

Yet Bert thinks Father can toss some holy water around and, what, dissolve one? For that matter, why was Father taking it so calmly? Are demons that weak here, or are Mundanes that deluded?

Father regarded me curiously, and I realized that not only was my mouth gaping wide enough for a family of cats to jump into, but that my wings were half-mantled and my back arched again. As I forced myself to relax, he said, "Easy, Vern. It's not like that in the Mundane. When demons prowl about the world seeking the ruin of souls, they don't do so in obvious physical form, nor do they possess fields or resort to actual murder."

"Hold on," Bert said. "You mean, there are actual, physical-type demons in Faerie? Could one of them have snuck in through the Gap?"

I moaned. The Gap was a single, stable interdimensional portal linking our universes. It doesn't move, doesn't close, and doesn't care what goes through it. The American military guarded the Mundane side. Duke Galen's soldiers, aided by Faerie Vatican mages, watch ours. It was unlikely anything evil snuck past, but we couldn't take that chance, could we? It could easily have hitched a ride on a less-than-honest sapient. Certainly, I've seen more than my fair share of those in my long life.

Maybe that's why I was Called here. If so, I was not a happy drake.

I took a deep, steadying breath. The Silent Brothers had healed me well. I could handle one demon. Maybe I could even work this to my advantage.

"If one did, will you deputize me to take care of it?" I cast a Father Rich a pointed look. May as well get a job out of it and make the priest happy.

Father rolled his eyes, and Bert snorted. "I don't think the county would go for that. But I wouldn't object to letting you ride along if you'd like to check things out unofficially."

Figures. Oh, well. At least it got me out of the garage and away from Crazy Cat Lady. Got to find that silver lining. That was about all the precious metal I got nowadays.

We piled into Bert's SUV. This wasn't the first time I'd ridden in the back of his police car, and with the seats folded down, it's a pretty sweet ride. It certainly beat most of the contraptions we have in Faerie. You'll find a lot of parallels between

Faerie and the Mundane, even to some of your political states, but technological progress isn't one of them. There are parts of Faerie—mostly in Pacific Asia and western Africa—that have entered what you call the Early Industrial Era: mechanical wonders run by a combination of steam power and magic. It's an exciting time for them, but I was stuck in a monastery in Faerie Britain, where the only thing pulling our plow was me.

Personally, I was perfectly content to skip over the whole revolution and enjoy the spoils. Electricity is its own kind of magic.

Bert stopped me from lowering the window. "Uh-uh. Last time you stuck your head out my car window, we nearly caused three accidents."

"What? So that's my fault, too?" I groused. First cats, now cars. Oh, and a demon who might not be a demon, but if it is, will probably want to go after me. This world was going to give me a complex.

Bert draped his arm over the back seat and twisted to look past me as he backed up. "Didn't say whose fault it was, but I can control your behavior easier than the rubberneckers'."

I did my best to content myself with the air conditioning and a view through the window. It wasn't much. Little Flower Parish was nestled on the poorer side of a town just starting to recover from decades of economic doldrums. We passed two long rows of rectangular houses Father called "trailers," each separated by its own chain-link fence, then larger, square houses, some with two stories. Some of the yards were neatly cultivated while others seemed to exist only to house rusting automobiles and fading plastic toys.

Bert took the exit, and the vista of peeling-paint patios and chain-link fences changed. We drove past and, thanks to the bridge, over, the railroad and warehouse district.

"So, what were you two arguing about, anyway?" he asked.

"Father thinks I need to get a job and move out of the garage," I said. Bert burst out laughing. Maybe he was imagining me in one of the trailers, navigating the narrow halls... I couldn't imagine it, myself. Would I have a nice garden or collect junk? Not that I have anything against collecting stuff—I am a dragon, after all—but my tastes run toward rare artifacts and precious gems.

And gold coins. Piles and piles of gold coins for bedding. I haven't slept well in 850 years.

Movement near a warehouse interrupted my daydream. My hawk-like eyesight was one of the first things God returned after George. Even so, with the speed of the car, I only got a glimpse of some teenage human in a black T-shirt jimmying a lock before we'd passed. I let it go. Even if I alerted Bert, we wouldn't get there before the kid had high-tailed it with whatever ill-gotten goods he'd grabbed. Besides, we were on the way to a murder and possible demonic possession.

Still, I made a note. Maybe I could find a job as a security guard. Probably be an easy gig compared to what I've done in the past. I wondered how it paid. Pre-George, most of my treasures were presented to me as tribute or exacted by me as punishment, and post-George, I was pretty much at the mercy of the charity of the Church. They'd made me take a vow of poverty and forbad me from visiting my treasure troves. I was stuck with charity.

The way Father Rich was explaining his side to Bert, I didn't think I could depend on the goodwill of the Mundane Catholic Church much longer.

"I'm not going to kick him out. But he can't live in the garage forever. He needs a job. He has to make his own way in our world," Father concluded, which for some reason, made Bert laugh harder.

I didn't find it funny. I had fully intended to make myself a home in one of the mountains, but the government prohibited it because I might somehow alter the environment of State Land. If anyone wanted to let me nest on their private property, they'd need to apply for appropriate permits, pay fees... The environmental impact study would take years, they said. I didn't even know what that was. I found myself continually amazed and bewildered at how a nation that allows so much license of bad habits allows so little freedom.

I looked out over the Rocky Mountains and tried not to feel wistful for my own home. Nestled in a cliff on the coast of what the Mundanes call Spain, I had a huge cozy cave, carved by some of the best dwarves in the mining industry. I bathed in the Medsea, hunted in the forests and plains, soared in clear blue skies. I went where I wanted, when I wanted. I made my own way. People came to me with petitions and rewards, and if the task were interesting enough or the reward worth the trouble, I'd grant the favor of my intelligence and strength. When I was challenged, it was a duel of courage and wit, not a passive-aggressive bludgeoning of bureaucracy.

If it's true that demons don't walk about the Mundane world, then I knew why. They're hiding in the offices creating new paperwork.

Father was tiring of Bert's snickers. "Look, all I'm saying is if Vern is going to be any representation of how the Faerie can adapt to our world, then he needs to make it on his own, not living off the charity of the Church."

"'He' is sitting right behind you," I groused.

"Yes, you are, and you are welcome to join in this conversation if you're done gazing out the window," Father Rich snapped. I had to hand it to him. Once he got over his awe of me, he treated me like any other parishioner, which meant I got scolded like the worst of them.

"I like going fast. I haven't moved this fast since I got transported to the parish. It's been weeks since I've flown."

My wings cramped, and I had a wild urge to burst out of Bert's car and take to the air. I quelled it. The last time I flew in the Mundane, I was circling the town, trying to get a lay of the land. Now, as a dragon, I was used to a certain amount of spectacle when I soar over unfamiliar airspace. But never had I garnered such ridiculous reaction.

Cars ran off the road or into each other. People either screamed or took photos with their phones. Then, some yokels came out with their guns. I might have been able to soar high enough that they'd never get me, but they weren't the smartest of shooters, and at the time, I didn't know how fast or far-reaching Mundane firearms are. I'd made a hasty and embarrassing retreat.

"Don't get any ideas," Bert warned. "It's only been a couple of weeks. Let people get used to you."

"When will that happen? What if I told you not to walk or use your hands for weeks until 'people got used to you'?"

Both he and Father sighed. I don't know. Maybe they hadn't thought about it, and yet, Mundanes understood flight. They have birds.

...which they keep in cages. Right.

"Just how am I supposed to be a representative of the Faerie when I'm not allowed to act like a Faerie? So far, I've been denied the right to make a lair for myself. I can't fly. And let's not forget the request that I be put on a leash."

"You have to meet us partway," Father started, but I cut him off.

"Which part? Next, I'll be expected to wear clothes."

Bert interjected, "All right, calm down, the both of you. You've got a point, Vern. Let me think about it. I might know someone who can help, too."

"That would be a change of pace."

Father's voice rose. "Excuse me! Who's let you live in his garage all month?"

Bert took an exit that led to a dirt road. The weeds and scrub oak turned to cultivated fields. Peppers, cantaloupe... Ugh, cantaloupe—the fruit directly responsible for the creation of the Interdimensional Gap and my current predicament. If I'd known cantaloupe were involved, I'd have stayed in the garage.

Like many Mundanes, Bert didn't like silence, even when he'd demanded it. "So, who are the

Silent Brothers? Sounds like a bad rock band," Bert said.

Father sighed. "Monks. They have a vow of silence."

"And you spent years with them?" Bert glanced at me in this rear-view mirror.

"A whole century."

"I'd have gone nuts after a couple of days. You really went a hundred years without conversation?"

"I needed the quiet," I started. Before he could ask why, I continued, "but when I got bored, I flew over to the Mercy Sisters' orchards. There's a wood nymph there. The sisters call her Euphrasia after the saint, but that's not her real name. Humans can't pronounce it. I'd go see her, call her name. She loved it. She'd make a whole field bloom in winter from the sheer joy of my visiting her."

Father let out a wistful sigh. "That'd be something to see. Would she ever come here, even for a visit?" As usual, talk of Faerie had brightened Father's mood. He was a serious romantic when it came to my universe. Sometimes, I wondered if I should take him over there, give him a tour, and let him be disappointed.

"She's two thousand years old. After that much time, she's completely bonded to her tree. I'm sure at some point, other nymphs will come looking for adventure."

"What could you possibly talk about with a nymph?" Bert asked.

"We have a lot of shared history." Of course, thanks to St. George, I'd forgotten pretty much everything from before around 1230, so she caught me up, plus taught me her language—a couple of them, actually. Her favorite was the language of the trees, something I was especially good at, since with my wings and long vocal cords, I could imitate the rustle of the wind and the groan of branches swaying in a breeze. That's why I didn't bother trying to say her name in the car. I didn't have enough room to move, and I wouldn't insult her by mispronouncing it, even in her absence.

Bert said, "Sounds like old ladies gossiping. There's the farm."

We pulled up to a side road that was blocked by a sheriff's car, lights off. The officer lounging against the hood stood up when he saw us. Another man in jeans and a jacket with the logo "McTaggert Farms" over the pocket halted his pacing and hurried toward us even before Bert stopped the car. His shoulders slumped in apparent relief when he saw Father, but my presence drew a completely different reaction.

"What is that...thing doing here?"

Something you need to know: Dragons are androgynous. We have no gender, but humans have assigned us each one for their convenience. However, I don't mind being called "it." But "thing," especially in that tone of voice, got under my scales.

"That thing is both intelligent and possesses excellent hearing," I chided. "As for what I'm doing here–"

The man turned to Bert. "I don't want it on my farm. The workers are spooked enough already. They keep talking about evil spirits."

"Mister McTaggert, Vern is here to assist."

"You're kidding me, right? Unless it's wearing a badge and comes with a court order, it's not setting foot on my farm."

Bert pursed his lips and tapped his fingers on his gun belt. I had only known Bert a couple of weeks, but I knew that stance. I'd seen it on guards when confronting some spoiled noble making a semi-reasonable request. And, in all fairness, it was somewhat reasonable. This was his land, after all.

At this point, Father stepped forward. He held his Last Rites kit out reverently. “Please. I was invited to minister to the body and bless the fields.”

“You, yes. The creature, no.”

I let out a sigh. If a Faerie demon was anywhere near the Host, they'd find out soon enough, and if I heard Father scream, I’d be on that land and to his defense whether they liked it or not. In the meantime, I jerked my head to a glen I could see peeking out between the trees. "How about I go relax in that meadow over there until you get things figured out. You can holler if you need me."

Of course, I didn't feel accommodating enough to navigate through the close-knit trees. With a great flap, I took to the air, just high enough to skim the treetops until I got to the clearing.

It wasn't big enough to be a field gone fallow. I saw a post with hooks, probably for tying up horses, and a packed-dirt area with a small fire pit. In Faerie, I'd have expected a serf's thatched hut. Here, I saw a plastic trash can with beer bottles and empty wrappers. It smelled of old vomit. I moved to the other side of the field. The end-of-summer heat and early fall rains had caused the area to explode in wildflowers and weeds. I settled down where the scent of flowers dominated.

I treated myself to a long stretch, extending each vertebra from neck to tail. I flexed my claws as if I were one of Dona Elena's cats. In the distance, I heard tires crunching on gravel as the two sheriff cars headed to the scene of the crime. I kept half an ear in their direction, but otherwise let the peace of the scenery lull me. The sun baked my scales with mellow warmth. How long had it been since I napped in a field of wildflowers? It didn't compare to gold, mind you, but it way outclassed the cement floor of the parish's garage. All things considered, I preferred these little flowers.

No one was watching, so I indulged myself. I circled my spot three times, deciding the most comfortable angle for sun and ground, and plopped down with my tail curled around me. I dozed, half listening in Bert's direction, just in case. At one point, I heard shouting, but it was human-to-human. None of my business, and I shouldn't go spook the workers, right? I roused myself long enough to make sure it wasn't anything more, then went back to my snooze.

A rustling in the woods heading my way woke me up in time to see a young woman burst through the trees and into my clearing. She stopped short when she saw me but didn't scream. Whatever had happened to her apparently propelled her beyond screaming. She sported a black eye, badly disguised by make-up, and the long-sleeved blouse in this heat told me she probably bore bruises elsewhere. Her hair was wild, her blouse ripped, and her eyes wide with fear.

But not necessarily of me. Or at least not just me. She stared at me for two breaths, glanced back the way she came, and ran in my direction.

That decided me. If something could scare a Mundane so much that she felt she'd rather face a dragon, she needed protecting. I let her dash by, and then leapt between her and the edge of the woods just as four men crashed through. I unfurled my wings, flared my cheek crests, and smiled.

At least, a dragon would know it was a smile. These thugs probably never got past the size and sharpness of my teeth to make a determination. One squealed. Another made a sharp rear march and retreated into the woods, proving at least one of them had a healthy sense of self-preservation. One, however, reached for his pocket. I'd already caught the scent of steel and could guess what hid there.

"Try it, Meat," I dared. "Let's see which hurts worse: your bullet or my fire."

He yanked the gun out of his pocket, anyway, and pointed it at me. I made a show of inhaling, and his grip wavered.

"Look, just give us the whore."

The girl had edged toward me. I didn't know if she recognized me as an ally or if she wanted to use me as a shield. No matter. I wrapped my tail around her. She shivered but didn't resist. There was more rusting in the woods, but I couldn't tell if it was cavalry for me or reinforcements for them.

"Why doesn't one of you take her place?" I suggested. I let myself drool for effect. As long as

Mundanes had ideas about what we dragons were, I might as well use it to my advantage.

"I'll shoot you!"

I didn't doubt he would—if he thought he could hurt me enough to keep me from hurting him. I needed to keep him guessing. "I wonder what happens when your bullet meets my flame. Think it will block it all?"

He hefted the gun, but still didn't pull the trigger. I nudged the girl out of his line of fire in case he got ideas about changing targets, but I released her from my grip. I hadn't been able to breathe fire since my altercation with St. George. If this guy didn't back down, my best bet was to risk getting shot and pounce fast in order to pin as many attackers as I could. The Church frowned on my biting off limbs, but with a little skill, I might slam him and maybe one of his cronies hard enough to knock them out. I bunched my muscles in preparation. Adrenaline coursed through my veins, a sweet feeling for a predator.

A deputy burst through the trees, followed by Bert. Both were fast on the draw, but the deputy, at least, didn't know at whom to aim. The muzzle of his pistol swung from the gunman to me, waiting for one of us to make a move. Everyone was waiting on everyone. It was a regular Mexican standoff, except not all of us were Mexican.

After a moment that seemed much longer, Bert stepped forward. "All right! Everyone calm down. Vern, relax. Kid, drop that gun now. You're not getting away, and you don't want to make this harder on yourself. Darren, arrest that kid for Carrying, and take the rest in for questioning."

With a couple of words I noted to teach Señora Costa, the guy tossed the gun and put his hands in the air, as did his buddies. Officer Juarez told them to get on their knees. My instincts called out, "easy prey!" but I quelled them and relaxed. I folded my wings but kept my attention on the trio while Darren handcuffed the leader, just in case any of them got ideas about running. At my back, I could feel the girl shivering. Typical damsel reaction after an encounter with a dragon, although usually, the damsel is shivering at the side of the knight. Out the corner of my eye, I saw Bert approach her.

"Teresa Ramirez? You're under arrest."

"What?" I twisted my head to get a good look at Bert handcuffing the damsel I'd almost gotten shot protecting.

Tears streamed down her cheeks and she sobbed. "No, no, no. El Señor, no."

The leader cheered, "Yeah! Lock her away. She's the real criminal. Murderer!"

Darren smacked him on the back of the head. "You have the right to remain silent, so shut up."

The girl kept sobbing, but other than speaking denials and prayers, she didn't resist. She wasn't in much shape for anything at that point. Bert had to hold her up as he led her away from me. Father ran from the edge of the woods to take her other side. From the way he glared at Bert, I had the feeling Father was thinking angry thoughts he should confess later. He put his arm around Teresa's waist to support her, and murmured promises in Spanish that they'd get everything straightened out. He never outright said it, but he obviously didn't think she was a murderer.

I didn't either. So, who was—and why would Bert arrest the wrong person?

Chapter Three: Fire and I.C.E.

We marched everyone back to the road, with Father and the girl far to the front, speaking in hushed tones, and Bert and Darren keeping watch over the thugs, with my help, of course. The cuffed guy kept silent, but the others didn't seem to care about what Bert called Miranda Rights. They alternated between accusing Teresa of murder and complaining about me.

"That thing needs to be in a zoo or something. It was going to burn us to a crisp! What's it doing roaming free, anyway?"

Another chortled and said in Spanish that stupid animals ought to stay mute.

"I think you mean 'dumb animals should stay dumb,'" I snarled, "and if you are going to pun, do it in the language that makes sense." Insults are one thing, after all, but badly executed puns really get on my nerves.

They went back to grumbling in Spanish about Teresa. I held my tongue, save the occasional growl when one of our prisoners looked like he was getting ideas about fleeing.

A sheriff's van waited at the road by the other cars. Our prisoners went in, with two protesting again that the girl had killed their friend. Darren took Teresa in his car. I'd have thought Father Rich would want to go with her, but he had other plans for our drive home.

Father lit into Bert as soon as we hit the highway. "You can't possibly think that poor girl did it!"

"She's the girlfriend," Bert replied reasonably, but he kept staring at the road. "She was last seen walking into the fields with him last night. She was hiding when everyone else gathered."

"She's terrified! And no wonder. You saw how those thugs went after her. They would have lynched her if Vern hadn't intervened."

"They think she's the murderer."

Father made an ugly laugh. "She's a victim. Did you see the black eye? It's older than yesterday. You know that as well as I."

"She has a lot of other bruises, too," I chipped in.

"You see?" Father exclaimed in triumph. "Even Vern can see she's been abused."

Bert shrugged. "Maybe she got sick of it and fought back for once."

"Right." Father flung his hand in dismissal. "And in self-defense, she shoved vines up her boyfriend's nose."

I'd seen humans kill each other in some creative ways over the millennia, but never like that. "That typical of Mundanes?"

"No." Bert puffed a sigh through his mustache. "Will you let me do my job, both of you? I'm not convinced she's guilty either, but a lot of people on that farm are, and they're willing to inflict 'justice' without my help. Even if she's innocent, this is for her own protection. And speaking of 'protection,' if you breathe fire on any human in this world, you'll get sent back to the Faerie in a cage, got it?"

I snorted. "It would be worth it. I haven't breathed fire in over 800 years."

"You were bluffing?" Father asked. I cocked my head at him, and he shook his, impressed.

"Why can't you breathe fire?" Bert asked.

I sighed. I'd rather talk about murder. "You can't kill a dragon, but you can hurt one—and most of our treasures are the ones we have naturally. Saint George took my fire, my size, and some of my magic. Most of my memories are hidden from me, along with just about everything I've learned over countless millennia. My abilities to sense everything from magic to smells are diminished. Everything about me is diminished! You Mundanes have been graced with a diminished dragon. If you met one of my kin, or me back before Saint George, there'd be no talk of sending me anywhere in a cage."

"Sorry," Bert muttered.

Father was similarly abashed. "You're not diminished, Vern. You're glorious. Maybe God put you in this state exactly so we Mundanes could handle being in your presence."

"I think you're all handling it a little too well," I grumbled.

There was a moment of silence, then Father and Bert burst out laughing.

Humans.

Bert dropped us off at the Little Flower parking lot. He rolled down the window and leaned out. "Listen, Vern, I have to get to the office and try to straighten all this out, but I was serious when I said I'd think about your situation. I'll introduce you to my friend Natura when she's back in town. She's a force for change, and she might be able to help you. If nothing else, she's gonna love you. Father, you're welcome, too."

Father Rich smiled. "She'll love Vern, indeed."

He waved as Bert drove off, but as soon as the car was out of sight, he turned to me, his face a dark cloud of anger. "There is no way Teresa murdered anyone, not even in self-defense!"

"She did seem more the run-and-hide type," I agreed.

"It's not just that!" Father continued, "Jace Keaton—the dead man—he's a big guy. He put up a fight. There were broken plants and trenches in the dirt where he kicked out. There's no way a frail thing like Teresa could have stood a chance. I mean, the murderer tied him up in vines! He choked him. He shoved plant matter in his mouth and his nose..."

Father cut off with a shudder.

It was probably a good thing I hadn't gone with them. I was hungry, and what Father described sounded like the dragon equivalent of a lunch wrap. I might have drooled, which probably would not have helped my reputation among Mundanes at all.

Father's fist clenched on the strap of his kit and he stared into the distance, probably still seeing the dead man. I put my tail on his shoulder and led him to the prayer garden. While he prayed silently, I stood watch. A couple of times, I saw tears dot his lashes, but they never spilled. I've seen a lot of humans who had witnessed violent death. His was one of the saner reactions.

Finally, he crossed himself and sat back. "Thank you. It was...gruesome. I understand why the workers were talking about ghosts and demons."

"And you're sure there weren't any?" I settled myself more comfortably on the stamped concrete. It had absorbed the late summer sunshine, and I enjoyed the warmth while I could. Harvest season was upon us. If something was in that field, every one of those workers was in danger.

Murders were usually personal; demons were only too glad to wreak widespread havoc in the most sinister way possible.

Father Rich grimaced. "If one of Satan's minions prowled that field, it didn't make itself known, even as I prayed over the body. I was going to bless the field, as much to reassure the migrants living on the property as anything, but we heard shouting, and then Teresa ran screaming from behind the shed with those boys in pursuit. She must have been hiding there all night. Vern, she's terrified. She thinks..." Again, he stopped.

"That she's to blame?"

"Worse than that. She thinks it was some kind of supernatural being, too—and that she called it somehow."

"Are you sure she didn't?"

"Vern, that's ridiculous! That kind of thing does not happen in the Mundane. She didn't do anything. She's just in shock. Survivor's guilt or something. I don't know." Father catapulted to his feet and paced.

Dragons have excellent vision, nearly 270 degrees. I didn't even move my head as he prowled from St. Mary by the roses to St. Francis by the petunias. I liked the statue of St. Francis; it bore a pretty good resemblance to St. Francis of Faerie. Good guy. He knew how to respect a dragon. He used to pace when he was agitated, too.

"She's innocent, Vern. She's innocent and abused, and now she's in a jail cell. Bert's right. She might be safer there than out where that gang can get her. But that poor girl!"

He paused before the Holy Virgin, as if hoping for her advice. Then he spun on his heel and faced me. "We have to prove her innocence!"

I tilted my head. "We?"

"Absolutely! Come on, surely in your millennia of life, you've solved a mystery or two."

The last "mystery" I had solved was to find and destroy an artifact that had been cursed to make a superweapon. That had left me a physical and emotional wreck for over a century. "I've never solved a murder."

He held out his hands entreatingly. "You're the smartest creature this side of the Gap. Can this really be beyond your skills?"

Of course, he appealed to my vanity. St. Francis used to do that, too. "Skills are not the problem. I'd have to ask questions, examine evidence, see the crime scene. How can I do that when I can barely leave the churchyard without an escort?"

His eyes lit up. "Let me do the legwork! I'll be Archibald to your Nero."

"Who?" The only famous Nero I knew had ruled Rome. He was a loon in our dimension, too. He certainly didn't have an assistant named Archibald. Not even his horse.

"He's a fictional character: a private detective who never leaves his home. His assistant, Archibald—Archie—did all the legwork: talked to police, checked out crime scenes, tailed suspects...though maybe I shouldn't do that part. But I can do the rest, and even better. I have this!"

He pulled out his smartphone. He went on about how he could take photos and recordings, but I was too busy envying to listen. One thing I love about the Mundane is its technology. Rumor had it that when the King and Queen of Tavendor made their historic visit to America, the President tried to give them a solar-powered photo frame with pictures of the visit, but the Queen insisted on a washing machine. It took two servants on bicycle-run generators to power it, and after the Queen ruined two ball gowns, she restricted it solely to the king's camping gear, her gardening frock, and the unmentionables of guests she wanted to impress. She loved it, anyway.

I have higher standards. That little box in Father's hand could hold enough information to keep me amused for a century, longer if I had Wi-Fi. If I had a lair here, I'd fill it with technology.

I must have sighed covetously, because his words slowed to a halt, and then his voice turned wry. "You know, if you were to help me on this case, we'd need to communicate. If we got you a tablet, we could Xinga."

"What's Xinga?"

"Communication over the Internet, audio and video and chat if we want. You get your own number, and if you have access to Wi-Fi, it's completely free. I would spring for a good tablet. I mean, if it's the best way for us to help Teresa..."

One of the first things I was told after my battle with George was that I would have to practice denial of material possessions. Not an easy task for a dragon, but what was the Lord's Prayer? Lead me not into temptation? Yet, here was His own servant, waving temptation at me like a red cape, as a bribe, no less. "Are you sure Bert will allow us to do his job?"

Father Rich scoffed. "We're not going to arrest anyone. I'm just going to ask questions, and you're going to use your superior mind to...help him out. It's a favor. An act of charity!"

"Who's your confessor?"

Father frowned. "I'm not going to sit around and let that poor girl face jail time or worse. Do you want the tablet?"

"I don't know anything about your Mundane laws."

He waved his hand in dismissal. "Right now, you just need to know a few basic, American laws and procedures. The other great thing about tablets is they can be eReaders, too. We'll get you some books about the law and being a detective. Oh! And the Nero Wolfe stories. Come on. It'll be fun!"

Dragons don't have hairy eyebrows to raise like humans, but I did my best imitation.

He blushed. "That didn't come out right. I just meant–"

I cut him off by standing and shaking out my wings. "I know what you meant. It's got to be better than having Señora Dona Elena breathing down my throat. Literally."

Father stuck his phone back in his pocket. "Yeah, what was that about, anyway?"

"She was looking for her cat."

"Down your throat?"

"And you completely underestimated my patience and self-control. What's our first step—after you buy me a new tablet?"

He cocked his head at me in exasperation and led the way back to the garage. "Much as I want to help Teresa, I have other duties, too. First, I have hospital visits. Then, if I have time, I can drop by the coroner before the Anderson funeral. Maybe tomorrow?"

"You'd better not be putting me off, Archie."

The smallest car I'd ever seen puttered into the parking lot and took the space nearest us. I don't think I could have fit in it even with all the seats removed. The back side declared it was "smart." Did that mean it worked on Wi-Fi, too? I caught a whiff of earth and fish when the driver opened the door to climb out. He dusted off his pants, knees and posterior, pulled at his cuffs, and approached Father with his hand out. "Good afternoon. I'm

Mark Fischer, Department of Immigrations." He gave me a cautious but otherwise cursory glance, the way someone might regard a behaving but unknown dog.

Father immediately stiffened. "Um, if this is about a parishioner, you have to understand..."

"No. Of course not. I'm here about your dragon." Again, the look flicked my way.

I was really getting tired of that look from Mundanes. "Well, Mark, let's start by making it clear that I'm not *his* dragon. If anything, he's my assistant. Aren't you, Archibald?"

"They told me you could talk English. I thought they were putting me on." He gave a short laugh, as if I'd done something amusing, and then turned his attention back to my friend. "Father Archibald, I wondered if I could ask you some questions."

"It's Richard. Vern was having a small joke."

I ignored his glare and did my best to look innocent. If I'd had eyelashes, I'd have batted them for good measure. I even refrained from saying that small jokes were probably the only kind Immigrations Officer Fischer could handle. However, I was anxious for my Archibald to get on with his mission. "Is there something I can do for you, Mister Fischer?"

Fischer cleared his throat, pulled at his cuffs again, and forced himself to address me. "Yes. Well. You see, there have been complaints."

I rolled my eyes so hard my neck arched. "I haven't eaten any cats—or small dogs—and if anyone's garden is in trouble, it would probably benefit from my 'visit.'"

"What? I'm talking about government complaints. Political."

If there's one thing I hate, it's getting caught up in politics. Politics are for lesser creatures jockeying for positions of power. Dragons were created to occupy the top of the food chain. I neither needed a politician's approval nor cared what politicians felt, and I told Fischer so.

His mouth twisted in annoyance. "Be that as it may, you are here, you are not human or even humanoid, and you present legal and political problems for our government. I've been sent here to evaluate you."

"Meaning?"

"The exact nature of your...classification under the law."

"Meaning?" I repeated with a little more force. I had a bad feeling about this.

Father Rich chimed in. "You're trying to decide if he's a legal alien?"

Fischer nodded. "He is from another dimension and came here without authorization. And no one in our world has seen a...dragon." He almost choked on the word.

I treated him to my most accommodating grin. If there was more than a hint of sarcasm behind it, I was sure he wouldn't notice. "Until now. You're welcome."

He turned back to Father. "I'm here to make an assessment of its habitat, behaviors, dietary requirements..."

I didn't mind being called 'it.' Dragons, after all, don't have a gender. If humans picked one for convenience, I had no objections. I did object, however, to being treated like a pet. I'd already done that phase post-George, and I was not repeating it for the sake of making a few politicos feel comfortable.

"Hey, Fischer. How about you show me yours, first? What's the natural habitat of the low-level government lackey here in the Mundane? From the crumbs on your suit, I'd guess your dietary needs run toward cheap pastries."

His back stiffened, but he kept talking to Father. "I understand you took this dragon in at the behest of the Catholic Church in Faerie. Were you given instructions or training regarding its care?"

"I'm not sure what you mean," Father said.

"Are there certain signals or commands to give it? Were you instructed in how to approach it?"

"How about with some respect?" I interposed myself between Father and Fischer. "If you have questions, you can ask me. That garage over there is as much my 'habitat' as a cheap hotel room would be yours. Then again, you're probably used to cheap. My dietary preferences are none of your business unless you are inviting me to dinner, and as for your thinly veiled references to obedience training, it seems to me you are more likely to jump through hoops at the bidding of your superiors. Do they reward you with fish? Because your car smells like trout."

Father put a hand on my shoulder, a plea for restraint as much as support. "Vern, there's no reason to be rude."

"Why not? I've been polite for weeks, and it's gotten me nowhere with your kind. But in deference to you, Father, I'll hold back. Just know this, Fischer: I am not an animal. I am a sapient being. My mind can think circles around yours. My knowledge spans centuries. My tastes are eccentric and wide ranging—and I am talking about art and literature as much as food. I make friends and enemies. I have a great sense of humor—but not today. So why don't you get back into your smelly little car, drive to your office, and write a report to whatever concerned politicians don't have the spine to come talk with me personally?"

Fischer's face grew a satisfying shade of red. "How dare you?"

"I dare because I can. Because it's what sapients are capable of doing. Now go. Father and I have work to do."

Fischer opened his mouth, closed it, and looked to Father. Father may have stepped out from behind me, but he backed me up, nonetheless. When Fischer saw he wasn't going to get any help, he spun on his heel and stalked to his car. The box on wheels barely made any noise as it started, backed up, and puttered out of the lot.

Father and I watched, silent and united, until it took a left and disappeared from sight.

Father's strong posture deflated. "I'm not sure it was such a good idea to treat him like that. Immigration has a lot of pull here now."

I shrugged, as much to release adrenaline as to communicate how little I cared. "Let him. At least now, he can't argue I'm not sapient."

I sauntered back to the garage. Sister Bernadette had left me a large bowl of water and one full of meat scraps from yesterday's funeral dinner. An apology, I guessed, for smacking me with the rake. I said a quick grace and wolfed down the contents. Only after I'd licked the bowl clean did I wonder what Fischer would have thought had he seen me.

Chapter Four: Dragon Gets a Job

Despite her peace offering, Sister Bernadette was not ready to have me around "polite company," and since they had the Anderson funeral in the church, she'd relegated me to Father's upstairs flat with the curtains closed. Father dropped by, in a hurry, but took a minute to point out the noir and mystery titles in his collection of old movies. Since I couldn't find any Nero adaptations, I started with *The Maltese Falcon* and moved on to *Casablanca*.

I may be a dragon, but there was something about the Bogart characters I identified with. I liked how he talked, too. Slang is a uniquely human convention. Few other species play with their words like humans. More than that, his attitude resonated with me. Like Rick Blaine in *Casablanca*, I, too, was an ex-pat with a past trying to make the best of a bum situation. Of course, my past involved a saint and not a woman, and Bishop Aiden would have a fit if I started a bar and casino. But that attitude... Yeah, I understood.

By the time Rick and Louis were walking away into a Casablanca fog, the funeral had ended, and the mourners were in the parish hall, sharing stories about the deceased over a hot buffet. I thought about Teresa, alone in her jail cell. Was she grieving her dead boyfriend or her own fate? I'd overheard her conversation with Father as we walked to the police cars—something I may have to confess later. She'd said Jace was getting rough with her in the field, and she'd prayed for someone to defend her. She honestly thought this was her fault.

I'd seen a lot of answered prayers in my lifetime, but never one that involved one's boyfriend getting both strangled and choked by the local crops. That was not how miracles worked.

Magic, on the other hand...

There was a miniscule amount of magic trickling through the Gap, which was a good thing; otherwise, Magical creatures like me could not live very long in the Mundane. We needed a small supply of magic to function. Unfortunately, the magic dissipated quickly in the Mundane environment, limiting just how far a Magical could get from our one tie to the Faerie realm.

Mundanes blamed themselves (or rather, other Mundanes) for not believing in Magic hard enough. Faerie experts think it's simply that the Mundane world is not meant to sustain magic, and no amount of clapping your hands saying you believe is going to bring a magic-starved fairy back from the brink.

Bishop Aiden had tasked me to test the boundaries of the magic's reach. Of course, since I'm not allowed to fly, that task is stuck on my growing To Do list. I could see the list in my head:

- [ ] Figure out why God sent me to the Mundane
- [ ] Earn the respect of the Mundanes
- [ ] Get a job
- [ ] Get a lair
- [ ] Test the boundaries of magic

...and now, Solve a murder.

What if God brought me here to solve a murder? I snorted. Nothing in my life since St. George has been that easy. It was even worse in the Mundane.

Since crossing the Gap, I've been under restrictions. My first month, I was detained in the military camp that guarded the Mundane side of the Gap. I was subjected to poking and prodding by Mundane scientists until they were confident I wasn't carrying any foreign diseases. I was interrogated as to my purpose, and yes, even my biological functions. Funny how a world that prided itself on its connectivity still couldn't get the word out that I could control my "biological functions" as well as any adult human.

I was given a list of rules to follow, which seemed to grow with every action I took. I was not allowed to do anything one of my kind would naturally do. And now, the government was coming to evaluate me—for what? Fitness to live among the Mundanes? As a Mundane?

Fine. I was going to have to play their game and on their terms. Just because I was an Eighth Day Creation didn't mean I couldn't slum for a while.

A lair, then, meant lodgings, which meant money. Respect, it seemed, also stemmed from money, to a degree, anyway. Father and Sister Bernadette certainly commanded the respect of their parishioners without possessing wealth, yet they also had a basic income.

So, money. Since, thanks to St. George, I was not allowed to touch my treasure—not that I wanted to sacrifice it just to please such an unappeasable species—that took me back to a job. Problem was, while people were nagging me about finding employment, no one was telling me how.

I tapped off the remote, then considered the technology I was holding. Did I need a human to tell me how to find a job?

I wandered into Father's study.

His computer demanded a password which I didn't have, but he'd left his phone on his desk, and I had seen the pattern he made with his finger before using it. The screen shifted from a photo of the parish to a plain blue screen littered with iconographs. I hadn't realized Mundanes used hieroglyphs, too.

I swiped a couple of screens, then saw one with the word Google and a white rectangle containing a magnifying glass and the word "Search" inside.

I'd heard Father talk about a search bar. It made more sense now. Gently, I tapped on the little keyboard, "How do I find a job?"

A new screen came up, with headlines in blue and a line or two of text beneath each, often cutting off mid-sentence. Since tapping seemed the *modus operandi*, I poked the phone with my claw and was rewarded with an article.

"Rewarded" being a relative term. The situation looked bleak even forgetting that I had four legs and a tail. I had Wisdom of the Ages—but no degree to prove it. I had fought armies, prevented wars, won battles of wits against the wisest and cleverest of the Faerie species (and yes, there is a difference between wise and clever). I had advised kings and paupers, protected popes... You get the picture. But go back as far as a century, and my job experience was pulling a plow for the Silent Brothers. I was not doing that here.

Especially if the crops were bent on murder.

I tapped the camera icon on Father's phone and pulled up the photos of the dead man that he'd taken at the coroner's. They were shaky and at odd angles. I suspected he took them on the sly.

Jace was a mess of bruises, abrasions, and chlorophyll stains. The vines were just weird. I could see a Mundane choking him with them, even stuffing them in his mouth. But up his nose? Threading them into his ears? Why take that kind of time?

Jokes about avenging-angel wood nymphs aside, it really did look like an attack a dryad might make. They could be vicious. Euphrasia, my nymph friend in the Mercy Sister's orchard, had killed a fox when it was trying to steal the baby squirrels nesting in her trunk. She'd skewered its brains, in one ear and out the other, and left it hanging for me as a snack the next time I visited. Vicious, yet thoughtful.

I couldn't see a dryad doing this, though. They were by nature gentle, and if they were going to kill something, it would be quick, like skewering the fox. This...this was messy, unbecoming, and dryads are nothing if not vain about their appearances.

Still...the only way to rule out nymphs or any other magical creature would be to go there myself.

I heard the downstairs door to the stairwell open and Father step in, talking to another man about civic duty and whatnot. I put the phone back how I'd found it, save for one little surprise, and headed back to the living room. When the door opened, Father found me curled up on the floor, innocently reading *The Catechism of the Catholic Church.*

Father did his best not to roll his eyes. He knew I'd memorized not only the *Catechism*, but also all the Mundane encyclicals back to Pope Pius X.

"Vern, I'd like you to meet Councilman Ripley Cliffman."

"Call me, 'Rip,'" he said, giving me a polite half bow in lieu of a handshake. "Father Rich and I have been discussing the problems you've been having adjusting to life here in Los Lagos."

"Odd topic of conversation for a funeral."

He had the grace to look a little embarrassed. "Well, I didn't really know the deceased. Mister Anderson was a well-respected pillar of the community, patron of the arts and education, so the council thought someone should officially represent the city."

"He was a good man," Father Rich added quietly.

The only time I'd seen Anderson, he'd pointed his cane at me and told me to stay away from his granddaughters. "He did have courage," I said.

Rip nodded. "But I must admit, I had an ulterior motive volunteering to come tonight. You see, unlike some of my fellow councilmembers, I think that we need to be doing more to integrate the Faerie into our community, and that includes you, Vern."

Now this conversation was worth having. I shut my book and sat up. "Does that mean I can fly again?"

He held up both hands. "Small steps, my new friend. There are still residents upset about the last time. But I was thinking there could be another way to get people used to your presence and get you out of the churchyard for a while.

"How would you like to be an ambassador for your kind here in Los Lagos?"

"Ambassador," I snorted at Father as he drove me to City Square. I was in the back of his truck with my head stuck in through the back window so he could hear me. "I've been an ambassador. This is more like a glorified talking circus exhibit."

"Quit breathing on my hair! Look, it's not much, I know, but it is a job. You get to hang out in the plaza and soak in the sun and answer people's questions."

"Like if I'm housebroken?"

He sighed. "I should make you confess your tendency toward pessimism...along with swiping my phone."

"I didn't take your phone. I put it right back where I found it, and I even left you a nice photo of me." In fact, it was a picture of the inside of my mouth with the caption, *See? No kittens!* "Besides, I was using it to find a job."

"And did you?"

"No."

"Then, be grateful. And stick your head back outside and enjoy the view. Weren't you just complaining yesterday about missing the wind on your scales?"

"Aw, you were listening!" With that, I did as I was told.

I have visited and lived in some amazing cities in Faerie. The elven village of Shyngciteeyon-dehyltatblinzfrumaffar is made completely from white marble. The elves—and most creatures that lived there—had developed nictitating lenses to protect themselves from the glare. Then, there was Dung, which was actually made of feces. Troll dung is sturdy stuff. It makes a solid home—if you have the olfactory fortitude to collect and shape it.

The truly cosmopolitan areas of my universe have similar variation in inhabitants. While my kind are as rare as we are beautiful, it's not too unusual to see a centaur skirting around some leprechaun who thought it'd be funny to start a rainbow in the middle of the road. (There's no end to a leprechaun rainbow, mind you. Two arches meet in the middle so both sides are the beginning.) Elves in long and flowing robes or practical woodland dress talking the human merchants glaze-eyed... Pixies and dwarves, even the occasional genie.

However, for sheer variety, a Mundane city outshines them all. Buildings of brick and stucco and something Father called “vinyl” that can look like wood but wasn’t. Signage in big, glowing letters, painted windows. Oh, windows! Faerie had just mastered pane glass in the past century, so to see it in so many shapes and sizes... Even the car windshields are a marvel. In fact, the very first travel book written by a Faerie about the Mundane had a whole chapter dedicated just to glass.

The sheer variety of vehicles on the streets is a marvel, too. It’s not that no one on Faerie would have the imagination to come up with so many different styles of chassis, it’s just that no one would think to bother. I’d mentioned it once to Bert, and he just shrugged and called it “capitalism at work.”

As for the human species, it seems standing out is an obsession with you Mundanes. We drove by a young woman with pink hair spiked high and bearing more tattoos than bare skin. I think I stared at her as much as she stared at me. Of course, she probably wasn’t wondering if all that ink made her inedible.

“There’s the historical district.” Father hollered through the open window and pointed to a large plaza surrounded by stores and businesses.

Those toward the street were occupied, but further back were more in various stages of construction. At the far end were the skeletal beginnings of a structure whose size would rival the Duke's castle. What noble was going to live there? In the center, a large fountain bubbled merrily.

Cliffman waited for us beside a sign declaring, "Los Lagos Historical District—the Charm of the Old West meets the Gap Age!"

"Welcome! Welcome!" He stepped to the curb and again treated me to a short bow before shaking Father's hand. He paused mid-handshake to turn Father's wrist to better examine the new watch adorning it. He whistled. "Nice smartwatch, Father!"

"Yes, isn't it?" I crooned sarcastically. After promising me a computer—as a bribe, even—Father had gone and bought himself a new tech toy first.

Not wanting to revisit our argument about his spending decisions, Father changed the subject to the renovations.

Rip pointed at the sign. "Like it? We're working hard to promote our motto: Past Remembering; Forward Thinking. You know there's already talk of changing the calendars from *ante diem* to Gap Age. That's how big the creation of the Gap is—and we're right here, on the edge of the frontier! Come, come—let me show you around."

He took us as far as the fountain and stopped. From there, he pointed out the shops that were open for business: a couple of coffee shops, a boutique, a souvenir shop with T-shirts bearing the city's motto, a store selling comic books and gaming supplies... It was still too early to open for the day, but I saw their owners watching me through their fancy painted windows. Only the comic shop owner seemed excited; he had his phone out and was tapping the screen.

"This has been my pet project for the past two years. It's still in the early stages, but next spring, the museum will be done, and this area will be flooded with families as well as tourists. It's such a boon for the town. This area was in sore need of renovations."

I looked at one building, boarded up with a For Lease sign in front of it, and wondered at the Mundane's idea of "needing renovations." Even the planks used to cover the windows were unlike anything seen in Faerie. Despite merely being wood chips held together by copious amounts of glue, they'd captured the attention of a Faerie artist who tried unsuccessfully to manually recreate the process of the machines. He finally gave up and went to the Los Lagos home repair store. Those $29.99 planks sold for a duke's ransom in Faerie Bordeaux. They graced noblemen's mantelpieces in Faerie. Here, they collected graffiti.

A scarecrow of a human with an ill-fitting uniform and a heavy utility belt that threatened to slide off his hips schlepped his way toward us. He gave me a disinterested look, then handed a paper to Cliffman.

"Barry Manns reporting for his shift. Can you sign this, so my supervisor knows I'm here?"

With a grin, Cliffman did so, then introduced us. "Vern, Barry here is going to work security for you."

I looked over my guard. Barely Man did not make me feel secure. "Is he protecting me from the humans or vice-versa?"

Cliffman laughed. "Think of it more as a reassurance for both sides."

"Security Theater," Manns muttered. He was eyeing a cardboard cutout of a scantily clad green woman that a worker was putting out in front of the comic shop. A fluffy, squat dog with a perpetual smile had followed him out and watched his master with devoted interest. The worker paused and waved at us. I jerked up my head in acknowledgement, and he gave a happy yelp and ran back in, the dog bouncing after him.

Cliffman continued, "This is going to be a slow week. School is still in session; people are at work... I thought it would be a good way to ease you into the routine. Before you know it, people will take you for granted, and we can dispense with the security officer."

Finally, Father spoke up. "Want me to stick around?" He didn't seem especially impressed by the security I was given, either.

But if I was going to make it in this world, I had to get out from the shadow of the Church. "I'm fine. Like you said, talk to people, soak up sun."

"All right, then." Father said a blessing over us and left with a promise to return at four. Cliffman made his goodbyes as well, with his own promise to return later in the day. Then it was me and my guard, who had already pulled out his phone.

Chapter Five: LARPing and Harping

For the first half hour, we sat in silence. I tried to start a conversation by asking my Security Thespian how much he was paid. "Not enough," was his reply, which made me wonder what the standard rate was for wearing ill-fitting clothes and sitting around watching your phone.

I entertained myself watching the shopkeepers watch me with trepidation. I heard some giggling in the comic book store, but it was all in a back room. Yeah, going to be a fun day. Most of the construction people entered the plaza by the museum side, so I got some distant stares and the perpetual phone photos. One person, dressed in a hard-plastic cap and yellow vest, came from the restaurant across the street. He stopped in front of me.

"Hey," he addressed my guard. "Is that thing real?"

I answered, "Yes, I am."

"Holy shit!"

"No, I'm neither."

He scurried away then, which was fine by me if that was going to be the extent of our banter.

I wasn't so lucky with our next visitor.

He, too, wore a hardhat and jacket and whistled as he swung his lunchbox. I'd have dismissed him as just another Mundane laborer, except that yesterday, he'd chased a young woman through the woods and into my protection.

When he saw me, his body jerked, then tensed. He headed to me with angry strides.

Barry noticed and prudent as always, decided to back me up from a respectable distance.

"Where is she?" he demanded as soon as he was close enough to talk without shouting. Guess he didn't want to be overheard in case any intentions of vengeful homicide slipped out.

"I think they call it, 'protective custody,'" I replied.

He cursed. "My friend is dead. His mom ain't stopped crying. The people on the farm are freaked out. But she's the one who's getting protected?"

"I'm sorry about your friend," I said, mostly to be polite, "but I doubt she could have killed him. And if there's something to be afraid of on that farm, get me access and I might be able to do something about it."

He shook his lunch box at me. "Just keep out of what isn't your business."

Was it my business? That seemed to be a matter of opinion—and everyone had a different opinion.

I jerked my head at his lunchbox. "Are you going to hit me with that or offer me a snack?" I asked.

He called me a couple of foul names, all less imaginative than Señora Dona Elena, and stalked off.

Barry returned from his "patrol" of the plaza. "What was that about?" he asked.

"I think he wants your job," I replied and left him to figure that out.

Since no one had bothered to provide me with drink, I helped myself to the fountain. I figured if anyone objected, I'd tell them Barry let me.

The doors to the comic store opened, and a dozen Mundanes stepped into the plaza. They were dressed in... I squinted. Was that supposed to be armor? It was made from plastic and a material that looked like leather but smelled synthetic. The chain mail was actual metal, at least. Some bore swords that even at a distance I could tell had never touched a sharpening stone. Even the little dog wore an outfit of thin metal and colored leather.

I poked Barry with my tail. "Can you explain that in twenty seconds or less?"

He glanced up from his phone. "Losers."

While I had no doubt they hadn't won any battles, that really didn't answer my question.

They stopped in front of me, crowded in a gaggle that said if there was a battle, they wouldn't win this one, either, and smiled, wide-eyed and a little maniacal. The last time I'd been given looks like that was from a group of dwarf children who came into my lair hoping I'd give them something so they could prove their bravery to their peers.

The tall one with short, dark hair and fake pointed ears stepped forward. "Great dragon of the Faerie Realm, I, Cirdan, Lord of Realm of Los Lagos, welcome you to our humble estate."

He bowed with a theatrical flourish of his hands. Under his chainmail, he wore a green T-shirt with an even greener man snarling out the middle of it.

"I thought Los Lagos was a democratic republic," I said.

Barry snorted. "Told you. Loser. Dressing up and pretending to be an authority figure."

I looked my guard over. Nope, he was not being ironic.

Lord Cirdan however, chuckled. "My apologies, uh..."

"Humans call me Vern."

"Vern. We didn't mean to confuse you. We're part of a LARPing—that's Live Action Role Playing—group called the Realm of Los Lagos."

Finally, the guy with the dog could contain himself no longer. "It's just so awesome that you're here! Oh, please, please, we'd be so thrilled and honored and totally stoked if you'd join our group."

The others made eager sounds of agreement. One in a pointed hat and robes pleaded for a photo as well.

Barry regarded them with a sneer. "Nerds."

"Geeks!" they chorused, then the one who asked for a photo added, "You know, Barry, you got no place to talk, making minimum wage."

Ha! There was that money-respect connection. I vowed not to let on how little I was making and instead took the side of—was he a mage? "Yeah, Barry. Why don't you make yourself useful and get a photo of us?"

Barry grudgingly agreed, and not one but five phones were shoved at him. We started with a simple crowd shot, but then they asked me to do some poses. I spread my wings, craned my neck, let them hug me. The other shops were opening, and while folks skirted around us, they did watch with curiosity rather than suspicion. When Lord Cirdan wanted to stage a battle, however, I declined.

"I have enough people with the wrong idea about me," I explained.

Suddenly, the guy with the dog—whose LARPing and actual name was Samwise—turned and stared at the restaurant across the street, where a young woman in a short skirt was wiping down the door.

The woman of our group, Lady Estel—whose real name was Linda—said, "For pity's sake, Sammy, go talk to her."

"Are you nuts? She's so out of my league."

"Glad to see you're smart enough to realize that," someone sneered from behind him. Everyone turned to glare at the young man who had a cup of coffee and a curled lip. "Why don't you be a good little nerd and stick with your kind? Rae belongs to me."

"Ew!" Linda said. "She doesn't even like you, Carlton."

"She does. She just doesn't know it yet." He gave them all one last disparaging look and sauntered off. He didn't even acknowledge my presence. Rude!

Linda stuck her finger in her mouth and made a retching sound as he crossed the street. "Ignore him, Sammy. Rae told me she can't wait for college just to get away from him."

"He's right, though. She's going to college, to major in marketing, like Fifth Avenue stuff. I work at the comic shop and sell computers at TechHut, and I make costumes for my dog. How can I impress her?"

"Hey! Thunderpaws is great! Girls love corgis."

Sir Balastar the Red—a.k.a., Ray—snapped his fingers. "I know! Vern, what if you kidnapped her?"

"What?" I was glad to hear others join my gasp of surprise.

"You know, like in the old stories. Then Samwise could stage a rescue."

There was a time in Faerie when such things were the trend of courtship. I had had a nice little scam going where I pretended to kidnap the princess and staged a battle with her intended—or suitors, if she didn't have one already picked out. I was well compensated for it, too. Somehow, however, I didn't picture the local authorities welcoming such schemes, and the last thing I needed was to get tossed in the zoo for playing matchmaker. "No. Find your own way to impress her. Try the dog."

I jerked my chin at Thunderpaws, who had wandered from the group and was entertaining some giggling teen girls in short skirts and shirts with LLH on them.

"Cheerleaders," Samwise sighed. "I'm doomed."

The rest of the morning went more slowly. The LARPing group returned to their—don't pardon the pun—Mundane jobs. A few people came by, but as Cliffman predicted, not many, and they kept to the edges of the plaza. Barry sat on the edge of the fountain and read his phone.

A disheveled man set up a wood crate not far from us, stood on it, and started shouting about the devil being before us. He didn't mean Barry. He read all the passages about serpents and dragons from the battered Bible he held in one hand. The cover said, "King James Version." I didn't know why the king had to have his own version, but I wondered if it left out all the parts where demons took human form, too.

"Hey," I hollered at him before he could work himself into a lather. "Read Job 41."

He stopped mid rant and gaped.

"Come on. Job 41. The Leviathan? That's my kin, you know."

"Be gone, Spawn of Satan!"

"What did you just call me?"

We both glanced at Barry. He was swiping at fruit on his phone. I looked back at the proselytizer. His gaze met mine. We smiled.

It was on.

"Let's start with Eve." This guy had a few verses about the serpent who tempted the human, but I had whole chapters about what that meant for all sapients. I rose and closed the distance between us, slowly, to give him time to flip through his king's book. He was going to need all the help he could get.

Just then, Councilman Cliffman came striding up. "Brother Zeke! What have I told you about setting up in the plaza? Do I need to call the police again?"

Apparently, fear of the police was stronger than his desire to extricate the devil. He jumped off his box and was gone before I could say, "In the beginning."

Cliffman continued toward me without acknowledging my opponent's escape. "So, Vern, enjoying yourself?"

"I was about to."

He laughed. "I have to meet with the foreman at the museum in about twenty minutes, so I thought I'd come see how things were going. Hey, Barry, you look like you deserve a break. I have a few minutes. Why don't you take fifteen and get something to drink?"

Barry took off almost as fast as Brother Zeke.

"What about you, Vern? Got everything you need? Hungry?"

"I'm fine." What I really was, was suspicious. First, a job, then arranging to talk to me alone, now the offer of food—no actual food, mind you, just the offer...

Mundanes were so awkward about offering me bribes. No matter: The bishop told me to be patient, so I'd wait to see what Cliffman really wanted, then suggest appropriate recompense.

He took Barry's spot by the fountain and pulled out what Father called an e-cig. I'd seen humans sucking on them. Cliffman just toyed with his.

"I quit smoking in January, but, you know, habit..."

I didn't get the connection, but I did know about habit. The first few years after George took my fire, I still reacted to threats by trying to breathe flames at them. It was kind of embarrassing.

"So... What do you think of our fair city?"

"That it hasn't been very fair to me."

He grimaced at that. "Yes, well, I understand, and you have a point, you really do. We need to learn as a Council and as a people which Faerie are trustworthy and which are a threat."

"There are some exceptions, but for the most part, the sapient races are pretty much like you Mundanes in that manner—blessed with Free Will and prone to temptations."

He nodded, but his pensive expression said that wasn't the answer he was looking for. "Yes, well... That murder was pretty grisly, I heard. You were there?"

I cocked my head innocently. What was he fishing for? "It unsettled Father Rich. I wasn't allowed onto the farm."

A flicker in his eyes said my statement clicked in his mind, but he brushed it off. "Well, it is private property, and a very busy farm. I hope the smells didn't put you off."

That was an odd hope, and I told him so.

"I...want you and your kind to be able to be comfortable is all. I'd heard that of all Faerie creatures, dragons have the most heightened senses.

I'd like to think we're developing a rapport. If you smelled any dangerous chemicals or sensed any foreign elements, you could say something to me." He stuck his e-cig in his mouth. He glanced around the plaza, trying to look casual while reassuring himself that no one was listening to us. The only person not engaged in commerce or eating was one twenty-something Mundane making his distracted way in our general direction while staring at his phone. What was it with Mundanes and those things?

Regardless, Rip seemed to think I was going to divulge some otherworldly insights. I may have been otherworldly, but I didn't have anything to share. "Rip, if it bothers humans, it'll probably bother most of the humanoid Faerie. I'd say the biggest concern Magicals have is the amount of iron in your steel and the need to stay near the Gap. Now, if you really want me to use my heightened senses to fully evaluate the area, I'd certainly be glad to. First, I need flying privileges back."

He blinked, pulled his e-cig out of his mouth, and stared at it. "I can't really do that. This is a...sensitive time, you see..."

"For whom?"

Abruptly, he stood. "I need to get to my meeting. It's been great chatting with you. And please—any concerns, anything you notice that's out of the ordinary... My door is always open to you."

Before I could protest that it wasn't anywhere near 20 minutes, he was hurrying away from me, his phone already out and his eyes down. He crashed right into the guy with the phone. Phones and the e-cig went flying. I shook my head as the two gathered up dropped items and apologized profusely to each other.

He headed to the museum, making a brief detour to send my keeper back. Report anything out of the ordinary, hm? I wondered if that included his behavior.

Chapter Six: No Good Deed...

I hadn't thought anything could make Barry lose that cell phone slump of his, but apparently all it took was a camera crew.

Once school had let out, people began to populate the plaza, and apparently the local news team—who had to have known I was there, since their building abuts the plaza—chose that moment to plan a spontaneous interview. Maybe they were waiting for a crowd; maybe they had timed it for a crowd, because as they were setting up, a bus pulled up to the curb and a group of people piled out, carrying homemade signs:

Dragon Go Home!

Earth is for Humans!

No Dangerous Animals!

It's my body! It's my choice!

One of the protestors pointed out that last one and after a brief argument, the woman holding it shoved it back into the bus.

"Are you going to do anything about them?" I asked Barry.

He tucked his shirt in for the third time in two minutes. "Free speech."

By then, the group was marching toward us—or if I judged the vector right, toward the best line of site for the cameras—while chanting, "Dragon go home! Earth is for humans." Good thing such shining prose was free.

The comics store doors opened and out marched my new friends bearing signs of their own. They began chanting as well: "Dragons are awesome! Vern is great! Why don't you can all your species hate?"

Ah well, they probably weren't getting paid, either.

Into this cacophony, a pretty lady holding a large mic smiled at the camera and began talking as if this had been going on all day.

Father had warned me, repeatedly, to be polite to any reporters I met, so while "Sarah Chiu, Channel 3 News" nattered on about crowds I never saw and excitement I hadn't caused, I surveyed our growing audience while trying to neither look threatening (easy) or annoyed (difficult). In addition to the protestors, there were mothers clutching their children's hands, people from the bistro clutching their drinks, shoppers clutching their bags...and one guy skulking among them nimbly lifting items that weren't being clutched tightly enough.

Was that the guy who bumped into Cliffman? Hope he checked his pockets when he got to the museum.

"Hey, Barry," I told my security officer, who was doing his best to look alert and authoritative while being neither. "There's a pickpocket among the crowd. Wanna go take care of that?"

Of course, right then, Sarah gave a flip of her hair and asked the camera, "How about if we find out from the horse's—sorry, dragon's—mouth?"

As she turned toward us, he stepped forward, his hands out, "Ma'am, I'll have to ask you to keep your distance."

"Why?" I countered. "You haven't all day—and what are you doing with your voice?"

While Barry blushed and clamped his mouth shut on his attempt to sound more masculine, the reporter beamed at me like I'd done a trick. "Oh! You can understand us!"

I'd been living among Mundanes for a month. I would not go so far as to say I understood them. "I can speak six languages fluently, seven if you count Mundane English. I don't remember how many I've forgotten."

I gave her the perfect opening for us to talk about my intelligence, but instead, she went to the obvious. "What exactly are you doing downtown?"

Just then, a woman screamed. She'd caught the pickpocket in the act, but rather than yanking his hand out of her bag and slinking away like a pro, he panicked and grabbed her whole purse, knocking her into the guy on her left. The thief took off toward the museum.

"Barry!" I said, but he just stared, surprised, as our thief gained distance and speed.

I should have just let him go, but my instincts were screaming, "prey!" and I hadn't had a good sprint in months. I bounded after him, right through the anti-dragon protestors. They toppled aside like tenpins.

I did not regret that.

I caught the purse gently in my teeth and pulled. The thief had a tight grip; his feet flew out from under him and he smacked the cobblestones with a satisfying thunk. I set a paw on his shoulder and leaned over so he got a good view of my teeth.

"Be a smart little human and stay still."

His eyes widened, then, defeated, he squeezed them shut let his head rest back on the ground. After eight centuries, I'd gotten very good at capturing humans unharmed.

I should have known the Mundanes would ruin my record.

People were screaming and stampeding out of the plaza. Others decided to defend the would-be criminal and pelted me with the handiest things available—which meant the detritus from the construction site. Rock, cement chunks and pieces of wood bounced off me and smacked my prisoner, who started wailing. I leaned over him to try to protect him.

Alarms sounded in the distance, but even worse, the cameraman was filming.

"Would you people calm down?" I said. "All I did was subdue a thief. Damsels and Knights! I didn't hurt him. Look."

I pulled back so that they could see his face. Some weenie-armed kid got him in the cheek with a badly aimed brick.

"Would you stop throwing those things?" both the thief and I chorused.

"Freeze, dragon!" Barry wheezed. He had finally made it to the scene and was pointing his squarish gun at me.

"Easy, Barry. I'm backing up. And you," I said to the human under my claws, "you stay right there."

That's when Barely Managing shot me.

Two little darts raced from his gun and impacted against my scales. I barely had time to register my confusion when lightning struck.

Or that's how it felt. I don't know what that little taste of Zeus does to humans, but dragons have some immunity against the elements. As it was, my entire left side froze, every muscle clenching, which meant the claws of my hand extended.

The hand still on the shoulder of my thief.

He screamed, of course. Then he started twitching.

"Stop that! Let him go!" Barry yelled, even as his hand pressed harder on the trigger.

Like I could. After that initial, involuntary contraction, every muscle on my left side froze, yet burned with a cold fire I'd never felt before. I tried to yell, but my vocal cords refused to obey. The pain was spreading to my right side.

Once again, instinct took over, and before the cold fire could engulf my head, I forced my neck down and bit at the wires connecting me to the gun.

Yeah. I'm going to start learning not to trust my instincts in this world.

Father Rich glared at me from where he sat in a cheap plastic chair. "Well, this is a fine mess you've gotten into."

"Me? This isn't my fault." I lisped because my tongue was still numb from being shocked. After my idiot attempt to free myself by biting down on the lightning cables, another guard added insult to injury by shooting me again in the jaw. By the time I'd finished twitching, they'd duct taped my mouth and bound my limbs with thin strips of plastic. *Then,* they made me walk to the security shack while they called Father.

I'd had to mince to the closet they called a break room. Not that there was much to break, just the table and two plastic chairs, plus a bulletin board with notices from something called OSHA and an infographic about how to spot and detain pickpockets. Apparently, siccing the resident dragon is not one of the approved methods.

I'd settled myself in the corner, cooperative and non-threatening. I even kept the stupid plastic ties on my legs. As soon as they'd shut the door and left us alone, I ripped the tape off my mouth. No one was denying me the right to talk back.

"Really?" Father replied. "Why did you have to tackle that kid?"

"He was stealing!"

"I know! And they carted him away in an ambulance."

"How is that my fault? I had him nice and quiet and *unharmed.* Then people started throwing bricks at us and I don't know what that gun was, but never show it to Thor."

Father moaned. "What am I going to tell the Bishop?" He lowered his head and started gently tapping it against the table.

"Tell him Mundanes are easily spooked and trigger happy. That's what I'm telling mine." I shifted, trying to get into a more comfortable position. My mouth ached and my gums had started to prickle. Something was wedged between two back teeth—a string or some tape, maybe. I tried to wiggle it out with a claw.

The door opened, and a tall, lean man in a suit strolled in. He had a badge on his lapel and a goofy grin on his face.

"I do hope that's not an escape attempt I'm witnessing." The jovial tone of his voice made me wonder if he was being friendly or hoping I'd break loose and bring some excitement to his day.

Before I could make a smart-aleck reply, Father said, "Captain Beavers! Andrew, please. This isn't what it seems. It's a huge misunderstanding!"

"Well, it's a little more than that," Captain Andrew Beavers, Chief of the Los Lagos Police, chuckled with an affectation of good humor. "We have a young man in the hospital thanks to those claws of yours, Vern."

"I never intended to do that. That happened because the security guards electrocuted–"

"Tased," Father corrected.

"Tased me. My gums are still numb."

Beavers gave a shout of triumph. "Oh! Is that why you sound like that?"

I held up my hands. "How about you undo whatever these things are."

"Zip ties," Father replied impatiently.

I shrugged impatiently. "Fine. Undo the zip ties, and we'll get out of here. You can even release the thief if you want. I'm going to bet he'll think twice before stealing again."

Captain Beavers made a theatrical sigh. "I wish it were that easy. You see, your ruckus made the news."

"Did it, really?"

"Vern," Father warned.

Beavers, however, continued as if we'd not spoken. "People expect me to do something. Some are saying you're a threat to the general public. A wild animal. Now I know that's not true. You're as sentient as I."

"Sapient."

"Pardon?"

"Sapient. Sentient beings have feelings and self-awareness. Animals are sentient. Sapient beings are capable of advanced reasoning. The Faerie have over a hundred sapient races, but you Mundanes only have one, not counting angels and demons."

Beavers laughed and slapped his knee. "See? You're smart, too. So, I'm sure you understand my predicament. Fortunately, I'm also smart, so if you'll trust me, I think I have an arrangement that will satisfy all parties and keep you out of trouble."

"And by 'trouble,' you mean your zoo?"

Beavers spread his hands and did his best to look pained. I didn't buy it. The pleading look Father Rich threw my way was genuine, however. How much trouble would he get into if I didn't cooperate?

I sighed. "Fine. What do I have to do?"

He let out a whistle, and like the Duke's hunting dogs, two uniformed officers, real policemen, stepped into the room. One handed him an odd device, a 3-inch square box attached to a wide strap of webbed fabric. Strap in his right hand, he draped the device over his left like a fine jeweler showing off an expensive bracelet. "All we need you to do is consent to wearing a little jewelry."

I gave him the stink eye. "You Mundanes have a strange definition of 'jewelry.'"

"No! Really, it's ugly, but it's state-of-the-art technology."

"Does it work like a smart watch?" I asked. Maybe that would give it some redeeming value.

Alas, Beavers shook his head. "It's more limited, I'm sorry, but it does monitor your movements and uploads the data to the cloud. Like a PhysFit."

I hesitated. I didn't understand half of what he'd just said, though I'm pretty sure he spoke English. What did clouds have to do with this? I thought state-of-the-art was a good thing, but what was a PhysFit and why would I like it? It wasn't like I understood smart watches, mind you, but at least I had a vague idea, thanks to Father's new toy. Speaking of Father Rich, he was refusing to look my way. Was he mad, or did he know something he didn't want to share?

"This is an expensive piece of jewelry we're entrusting to you, Vern. We're just asking that you wear it."

I did like expensive things, and I didn't really see any other way out of here. I sat back on my haunches and held out my front legs again. The officer stepped forward, cautiously, and snipped the plastic zip ties binding them. Then he did the same with the back ones. Next, he strapped the PhysFit-like thing to my left leg, using a red tool to secure it in place. A light on it flashed. That was momentarily interesting, at least.

Beavers must have caught my expression because he clapped his hands in triumph. "You see? Everybody wins! Now, one last, teensy favor. The reporters are waiting."

"What?" Father exploded.

Beavers held out his hands in a placating gesture. "It won't be any trouble for you or the parish, Father. We're just going to go outside and show everyone Vern's new bracelet."

Father sighed but waved to the door.

We followed Beavers out, the uniformed officers behind us.

A mob waited for us outside, but at least they only wielded cameras and not sharp gardening tools. The reporters were interviewing them or filming the scene of the incident, which was now cordoned off with yellow tape that said, "Crime Scene: Do Not Cross." Since there wasn't any crime, I was feeling more crossed—and cross—by the minute.

A couple of guys in green coveralls were picking up broken pieces of masonry while the security guards bragged about slaying a dragon. When they saw me, Barry's compadre used two fingers to point at his eyes, then at me. I gave him a smile that was full of teeth. He went pale and swallowed hard, but he didn't wet himself. Had to give him credit for that.

As soon as the doors closed at our backs, the reporters left their conversations and swarmed toward us. Cameras and microphones pointed in our direction, and questions flew too quickly to get answered.

Captain Beavers smiled and raised his hands. "Friends! Friends! There's no need for alarm. I'm pleased to announce that I have brokered a peaceable settlement. Really, it was a simple misunderstanding that got out of hand."

"That dragon trampled us!" shouted one of the crowd. I recognized the protester from the bus. "What right does he have chasing humans?"

"It was a thief, and I only tackled him!" I retorted. "My body, my choice, lady."

I felt a sharp pain in my tail as Father Rich stomped on it.

Beavers set a hand on my flank. "It was indeed a pickpocket, and my fine officers have taken him into custody pending his release from the hospital. Meanwhile, our dragon friend has agreed that in return for not pressing charges against him–"

"What? What charges?" I demanded. Behind me, Father stomped on my tail again, then held his foot on it. I couldn't jerk it away without toppling him, and he knew it.

Beavers laughed. That jovial guffaw was getting on my nerves, just like that way he had of touching my shoulder like he owned me. "Exactly! But to reassure the public, Vern has agreed to restrict his movements in our world."

"I have?"

Stomp!

"Fine. Sure. I have. For now, anyway."

Beavers smacked my shoulder then rubbed the spot. "What a sport, am I right? And to be sure we are all in accord, he will wear an ankle monitoring device. We will be able to track his movements in our fair city, and if he should stray beyond the grounds of Little Flower Parish, rest assured the LLPD will be on the scene to ensure the safety of all!"

With that, he grabbed my leg, nearly toppling me as he held it up for everyone to see. I heard the snick-snick-snick of dozens of cameras. Behind me, Father Rich applied pressure with his foot. I gritted my teeth and held my tongue as people took my picture and Beavers ignored their questions.

But I did not smile.

Chapter Seven: Parish Grounded

The next morning saw me back to my same, tired routine. I awoke before the sun to take care of my personal needs out of sight of parishioners and nosy neighbors. Then I listened to daily Mass from within the closed garage. Afterwards, I joined Father and Sister Bernadette for breakfast on the back porch, also away from the prying eyes of neighbors.

Despite Sister's rule about no cell phones at the table, Father pulled out his and slid it to me. "Rip texted you last night. Twice."

I looked at the screen:

Vern,

My apologies. You Are not to blame. Don't give up on us mundanes. Everything will work out in the end. Rip.

And an hour later:

Vern,

Again, apologies. Very sorry. Everyone isn't against you. Never give up! Get out there and solve this. Even with these setbacks, you can do it. My faith in you is strong. Everything will work out.

Sister Bernadette peeked over my shoulder. "He really took it hard. Poor man."

I didn't reply. In Faerie, especially before St. George, if I'd been doing something for another sapient and ended up in a mess like this, there'd be groveling and tribute. Of course, if I were in Faerie, this would never have happened.

"I tried to text him back, but he's not answering." Father started to put the phone back in his pocket. Sister Bernadette stopped him.

"Would you like to text him a reply?" she asked me in that pointed way mothers and nuns had that said, "Yes, you would, if you know what's good for you."

"I'd rather talk to him in person." Forgiveness was best done face-to-face, after the other party has sufficiently groveled, of course. But Sister Bernadette's expression darkened in that way St. Joan's used to, and I knew I'd regret winning this argument. I took the phone and tapped out a reply, along with an invitation to come over and discuss it.

Father looked at it and frowned, but all he said was, “He doesn’t acknowledge seeing it, just like mine.”

“He may just be busy,” Sister consoled, and moved the conversation. “We visited Teresa yesterday, Vern. She wanted us to thank you for protecting her. Someone posted her bail, and they’ll be moving her to a safe house this afternoon, just in case there are others who blame her for the death. I plan on bringing her some clothes.”

Father sighed as he put his phone in his pocket. “After yesterday, I doubt we’re going to have much chance to find the killer.”

Sister Bernadette sat back and crossed her arms. “Teresa is being released. You do not need to prove her innocence. I’m relieved. We have enough trouble right now without you two finding more.”

I shrugged. I hadn’t gone looking for trouble in over eight centuries. Trouble usually came to me.

As predicted, trouble came again late that afternoon.

I was snoozing in the garden, half-hidden among some aging spruces, when the Trio of Trouble approached. Bert was in civilian clothes and wore cologne, but his expression was anything but sociable. Not that I blame him, since Agent Fischer from Immigrations was with him. Father trailed behind, looking almost as sick as he had after viewing the dead body.

Bert said, "I'm off the grid one day..."

I'd already decided to accept my punishment like a good martyr, but that didn't mean I was going to take the blame, especially in front of Fischer. "If my 'security guard' hadn't been as lazy as he was trigger-happy, I'd probably be at the plaza again making friends and getting paid. Maybe you should be talking to Cliffman."

"Cliffman's dead," Fischer snapped at me.

I'd already been planning a snark for whatever he threw at me, but that one stopped me cold. I glanced at Father. He nodded. Fischer continued to glare at me expectantly.

"I didn't do it," I said.

Bert replied, "He did it to himself—drunk driving, speeding on a dangerous mountain road. He missed a curve and plummeted off the edge. If one of my deputies hadn't seen the damaged railing, we probably wouldn't have found him."

Fischer shot him a dark look. "And yet, how interesting that he chose yesterday to get drunk. And Father here tells us he sent you not one, but two apologies. What have you to say to that, dragon?"

"I'd say that that's evidence that an official of your government recognized me as a person rather than an animal."

His face reddened in the same satisfying way as it had the last time we talked. I might have to start keeping score.

He didn't give up his attack, however. "There is a traumatized young man on a bus to Denver this very minute, despite his injuries, because he's too afraid to stay in Los Lagos. You should be in a zoo for the trouble you've caused."

"I caused? That kid was perfectly safe until Security Man decided to zap me."

"–but Captain Beavers had to make a show of treating you like an intelligent being..."

His voice trailed off, and his eyes got wide. That's when I realized I'd stood up and unfurled my wings. Even at a sixth of my size, I was a scary sight when I got mad.

It was probably not the best reaction I could have had, but the damage was done. Might as well use it to my advantage. I stretched to make myself even taller, then leaned my head down until it almost touched his. Fischer froze under my glare.

"Try me, human," I growled.

"W-w-what?"

"Try me. I would match my intelligence against yours any day. Even with all the wisdom and knowledge that God and Saint George have taken from me, you're still no match for me."

"I don't understand."

"I'm not surprised. Maybe when you do understand, you'll realize I'm not an animal nor an idiot. I am, however, in possession of a very sharp mind as well as sharp claws."

"Are you threatening me?"

"No." Now that he was sweating, I slowly and deliberately settled down. I flicked some dirt off one of my very sharp claws before retracting them and continued. "No. I'm stating a fact. I haven't threatened anyone since I've been here, and that has been a heroic feat of self-control. I have taken down a pickpocket, whom you've just told me has been released despite his crimes, while I was hit by rocks, tased, and am now confined to church grounds where people like you can come and insult me. My patience is running thin. So, if you want to have a battle of the wits, then let's do it, but remember: When I win, I expect a prize."

I must have drooled a little by accident. He backed away from me, slowly, never taking his eyes off me, but not quite making eye contact. Once he'd gotten out of swiping range, he turned to Father. "We're not through here. Get that creature under control," he said. Then he stormed away.

Instead of responding to his lame excuse for last words, I turned to Bert. "They let the thief go?"

Bert shrugged. "Beavers said the kid lawyered up before he even left the hospital. He got a plea bargain. In return for giving the police everything he stole, they dropped the charges and let him go. He really did ask to be on the first bus out of town. Who knows? Maybe he learned something. The question on my mind is, have you two learned anything?"

"That we should have 'lawyered up'?" I ventured.

Father sighed, but I couldn't tell if it was with exasperation or guilt.

Bert smoothed down his mustache while he thought. Then he shrugged. "We're not letting this ruin my plans, and you two look like you need some good food and a new perspective. I know where you can get both."

Father regarded him with a raised brow and a downturned mouth. "Us two? Someone can't leave the parish grounds."

"Let me handle that. Would Sister B want to come?"

"Nah, this is her night to get away from her little brother and hang out with the other Salesian Sisters in the area. They're meeting in Cañon City tonight."

"Okay, go lock up and meet us in the car. Let's go, Vern."

I followed dutifully to the car, but once in, I started with my own questions. "'Not messing up *your* plans?'"

"I said the other day I wanted you to meet someone, didn't I?" He tried to sound casual, but there was just enough defensive inflection to tell me his plans were more personal than that.

"Is that why you're all dolled up?" I'd learned the slang watching more noir movies. It was apparently the perfect phrase for the occasion; even from the back seat, I could feel his skin heat up.

"I don't wear my uniform all the time, you know."

"Of course not," I agreed amicably, then, "You smell nice, too."

Father's arrival spared him from having to reply. "Did he explain to you how we're supposed to leave the parking lot without getting arrested?" Father asked as he shut the door.

"No, we were just getting to how sprucing up worked into the plan."

Father smirked. So, there was something going on! But the smile faded into one of innocence as Bert rolled his eyes and grabbed the mic for his radio.

"City Dispatch, this is Sheriff Wheeler. I'm taking the dragon Vern into my custody for questioning, copy?"

There was a pause.

"Repeat that last, Sheriff: You are taking the dragon off parish grounds?"

"Temporarily, yeah. For questioning. Might get dinner, too. I'm sure Captain Beavers won't have a problem with that."

This time, the radio seemed to squawk disapprovingly. Then, "Los Lagos Dispatch to Sheriff Wheeler: Vern the dragon is temporarily remanded to your custody."

Bert grinned at us. "Roger, Dispatch. I'll have him home around 2100 or so."

Bert pulled out of the parking lot. As he turned the corner, I caught a glimpse of Señora Dona Elena la Gataloca hobbling down the street, a can of tuna precariously held by thumb and forefinger while the other fingers gripped the handle of her walker. She was calling Sacha's name, oblivious to the five other cats who followed her meowing.

Father said to Bert, "That's it? After the big deal Captain Beavers made about this agreement, you just call in, and they ignore it?"

"Beavers knows what's good for him."

"What does that mean?" Father asked, and I turned from watching Crazy Cat Lady because I wanted to know, too.

Bert sighed. "Andrew Beavers is more interested in being popular than in protecting his people—his cops or the people of the city. Not been much of an issue with Los Lagos being so small. Most of the time, we deal with petty crime or something open-and-shut, like a domestic that leads to murder. A domestic is a fight between husband and wife, Vern. Beavers is actually pretty good at the diplomatic stuff. He's helped more than one fighting couple find common ground and make peace. Still, if something gets complicated and the city's been too 'understanding," his people come to me, and we find a county connection to make good on an arrest. My guys do the dirty work, and Beavers gets hailed for his skills in interdepartmental collaboration and takes credit for the city's low crime rate."

"You don't like him much." I observed.

"With the Gap connecting our worlds, Los Lagos is going to grow, and fast. That means crime is going to rise. Beavers won't be able to handle it.

And I ain't retiring until we have someone in who can."

"You want to retire?"

"I've been sheriff for twenty-five years and a deputy fifteen before that. I'm ready for a change. But not until the city has a real chief of police. If this place goes to hell, it will drag the county along with it."

We reached downtown and passed by the City Square of Entrapment. The shops were open and doing pretty good business, even the comics store. I saw a sign in their window: FREE VERN. Not all Mundanes were bad. We went past, then Bert took a right up a side street, then another up an alley. We parked in the alley behind the restaurant, next to the dumpsters.

"I hope that's not my dinner," I remarked, twitching my nose at the smell.

"Relax. Natura has something special planned for you." Bert led us to the back door.

It swung open before his hand touched the knob. Amazing smells wafted forth, making me completely forget my snark about the dumpster. In the doorway stood an appetizer-sized woman in a flowing, multicolored frock. She held the door open with one flat palm while the other was planted on her hip. The security light above the door lit her graying blond hair like sunshine but did little to soften her frown.

"I told you to use the front door!"

"And I told you it was a bad idea to parade Vern through the front."

Bert had taken an unconscious step forward as he'd said this, and slay me if I couldn't smell the pheromones and frustration. I glanced at Father Rich, who was suppressing a grin. So, this was a long-running thing, then.

Bert had followed up his argument. "It's not that I don't sympathize, but I have a reelection coming up, and I'd like to keep my job. I can't afford to play favorites."

"Favorites!" she snorted. "Vern has been badly mistreated. You uphold the law of the humancentric patriarchy, sure, but you always find a way to stand up for the rights of the oppressed. That's what gets you reelected."

"Not if I rub it in Beavers' face."

She rolled her eyes at him, but he'd made his point. Tender moment completed, she swooped past him, leaving him to catch the door, and made a beeline to me.

She smiled at me as if she'd been given a great gift. "Oh, Vern! Namaste! Welcome, welcome. Please, come in—enter a domain of acceptance and agape."

From the door Bert said, "*Ah-gap-ay* is all well and good, but I think he's more interested in a full *bell-ay*. I think I heard his stomach growl."

He was right. The smells wafting through the door were tantalizing. "I do smell masala," I said.

"So do I," Father interjected.

She laughed and took his hand. "Then, come! I have reserved the Safe Space Lounge just for us." She led the way, moving with a graceful ease I seldom saw in women her age. As she passed Bert, she gave him a grin that was both grateful and admiring. Bert played it cool, but I understood. This visit was not about showing me kindness. This was about impressing a female.

I've been part of courtship shticks before, but never as the offering.

"Natura," I said as I entered the restaurant. "What do you have to drink here?"

After all, I don't come cheap.

Chapter Eight: Visit to a Safe Space

I didn't notice any extra security in the Safe Space Lounge. Instead, walls of multicolored patterns bore stenciled messages:

YOU ARE SAFE HERE.

YOU ARE LOVED.

YOU ARE ACCEPTED.

BE YOUR TRUE YOU!

A portion of one wall was painted black, with an invitation to "write your own self-affirming statements." A pedestal held a dish with chalk. Over the speakers, someone was singing about the wind blowing around answers to riddles. The Sphinx would have liked it; she's always looking for new material.

Plush chairs around small tables dotted three corners of the room. In the center were longer, shorter tables with pillows a dwarf could comfortably nap in. We went to one that already had one side cleared of pillows for me. I'd have expected Bert to balk at the cushions, but he settled in with the ease of someone who did a lot of floor sitting. Menus lay on the table, but my nose had already told me what was available. Besides, the "true me" was a hungry dragon with expensive tastes.

A waiter immediately entered, and I gave him my list, ending with four of their most expensive beers.

Bert nixed that order, changing it to some local microbrew. "Trust me on this one, Vern."

While we waited for food, the humans made small talk. Natura told us about her walkabout, which didn't involve walking as much as driving to places at random while asking herself, "Who am I now?" She ended up at something called Soulfire, which she described as "Burning Man, but more spiritually satisfying."

"Not literally burning, Vern," Father explained when he caught my expression.

I hid my disappointment. For a moment, it had sounded like someplace I could have been my true self.

"You wouldn't like it," Natura said. "It's become so conventional. Soulfire let me open myself to my essence. That's when I felt my Calling."

The food arrived then, and conversation stopped as we dug in. The tastes lived up to the promise of the smells: rich and heavy, creamy, and sweet. The vegetables had a...something...to them that was unlike anything I'd tasted in the Mundane world, yet enticingly familiar. I asked for seconds, then thirds, plus more beer to wash it down.

"Hey," Bert protested, "I said I'd treat you to dinner, not all the food in the restaurant."

"Leave him alone," Natura said. "It's probably the first time since crossing the Gap that he's been able to enjoy a truly organic meal. Speaking of organic, may I ask an indelicate question?"

Bert nearly spat out his beer. "No! You are not discussing dragon...scat...at the table."

"Fewmets," I corrected. "The proper term is 'fewmets.'"

She smiled at Bert. It almost seemed pitying. "You are so uptight. Night soil—or fewmets, in Vern's case—is a fully natural resource and in many cases, excellent fertilizer. But it's cool. The

Safe Space Lounge is all about finding mutually comfortable topics of conversation."

Her voice got fierce. "Let's talk about the supreme injustice foisted upon one who should be the most honored guest of our dimension."

"I'm comfortable with this topic," I said through a mouthful. "Continue."

"Vern, on behalf of the human race, I apologize. If only I'd been there, I'd have started a protest for your freedom."

"There was a protest," Father said with a sigh. "Which attracted the pickpocket and led to the trouble in the first place."

"All I did was catch him," I said.

"You punctured him with your claws."

"Not my fault. Officer Barely Man tased me."

"You see?" Natura pounced on my statement like a cat—or a dragon. "Police brutality. Another example of jackbooted thugs hired by the government and given authority they can't handle responsibly. No offense, Bert."

"None taken. He was a rent-a-cop."

"Hired by our city council! And where was Councilman Cliffman? Why has he not taken responsibility and stepped forward to end this injustice? I expected better of Rip."

"Nat," Bert said gently. "He's dead. Drunk driving, missed a turn."

"What? No."

"I'm sorry, Nat."

"No," she said, crossing her arms. "He would not have been drunk, not Rip."

"I'm sorry, Nat. I know he was one of your 'projects,' but Darren found his car. There was alcohol on the scene."

"Then they need to do an autopsy. He couldn't be drunk. He's been sober since his fourth DUI."

"He's only had three."

"Right. Because I didn't report the last one. Oh, don't roll your eyes at me. He needed rehabilitation, not incarceration. Besides, after he almost ran me over–"

"He *what?* Natura!"

"Chill. I just got a couple of bruises. Worth it, because it totally scared him straight. He started AA, and with that and the acupuncture and total dietary detox, he was clean for the first time in his life. He's been living clean since January. It was his religion! He'd never go back."

Father said, "Maybe this incident drove him over the edge." He handed her his cell phone.

She read the texts. "This proves it. No one drunk texts like this. Besides, I'm telling you, control was his new drug. I mean, healthy living is groovy, but it was a full-on discipline trip for him. It was worse when he was stressed, and he'd been under a lot of stress lately. I could tell, because before I went on walkabout, he was all over me about my food and where it came from. I told him, 'Lay off, man. You can totally trust me,' and he was like, 'but who do you trust?' He even texted me, asking what farms I got my produce from, but he'd never tell me why. I said we'd talk when I got back—if I got back. I mean, the point of walkabout is to rediscover yourself, and what if I'd decided I was someone else now?"

"She has a point," Father said, taking back his phone. "The English is almost perfect. Stilted even."

"Like someone else was texting, thinking that's how he'd write?" I asked.

Bert was good at his job; he caught my line of thought and reeled it in. "You think someone else had his phone and did it to make it look more like suicide or a remorse drinking?"

"That pickpocket did bump into him earlier, but he didn't say anything about missing his phone."

"He might not have noticed," Father added.

Bert nodded. "It's a longshot, but I'll make sure the investigators know to check it out. We'll need screenshots of those texts, too; don't forget."

One of the waiters approached us. He cleared his throat. "Sorry, Natura, but... He's back."

From the tone of his voice, "he" was a longstanding problem for Natura. Bert picked up on that, too. "Need any help?" he asked.

Natura opened her mouth as if to protest, but instead, she said, "If I need the Heat, I'll holler."

"I can't breathe fire anymore," I told Bert as she left with the waiter.

Bert snickered and shook his head, but he asked, "Can you listen in, just to let me know if she wants some support from 'the Heat'?"

God may have taken away my flame, but He had seen fit to return to me much of my dragon senses. You'd call them advanced, I'm sure, but trust me, they are still sub-standard compared to when I was in my prime. Still, I could hear the conversation as she argued with a young man. Even better, if I stretched my neck a little, I could watch through a gap in the beaded curtain that covered the door she'd left open.

The young man leaned against the hostess station, staring at a dark-skinned young woman whose thin, muscular body fit the description of attractive in the Mundane. I recognized the girl as the one Samwise had been sighing over, Rae. Unless she was just unlucky, that made the troublesome guy the one who'd declared her "his." I thought I'd recognized the voice.

Rae's eyes darted from Natura to the man, and when he winked at her, she glared back, but pressed the stack of menus more firmly against her chest. She stood half a pace away from her own podium.

Natura spoke earnestly to the young man, but he turned his gaze away from the hostess only long enough to smirk or roll his eyes at what Natura was telling him.

I had been around mortals enough to guess at the situation. I'd seen it in taverns and feasts. A young noble sets his eyes on a lovely serving girl and in true nobleman fashion, thinks his wealth and station have earned him certain attentions, regardless of how the girl feels. Whether or not this kid was whatever passed for nobility in a democratic republic was a mystery to me. His clothes didn't seem especially rich, but Sister Bernadette had explained to me that some people paid the price of a suit for a T-shirt.

"Rae is a strong, independent woman, not someone you can dominate, anyway," Natura concluded as she tossed her hair. "Why don't you go back to the country club and find someone there who might be impressed by your daddy's bank account?"

He sneered. "Why don't you butt out of my business? I was talking to Rae."

Rae responded in clipped tones. "And I told you I'm not interested, just like I told you yesterday, and the day before."

"You'll come around, hot stuff. I'm nothing if not persistent."

Now, Natura lost her temper. "That's it. Get out of my restaurant."

He snorted. "Or what? You'll call the police, have me arrested for talking?'

"I'll throw you out personally, *personally*, and then share the security footage of the event on Flôwer. Trust me, your daddy's lawyers can't fight the embarrassment of social media. Not to mention, this is Natura's—the most diversity-embracing restaurant in the state. Think hard, Carlton. You are privileged, white, and male. How's that going to look when people see you sexually harassing a young African American woman?"

His face flushed, and he spun on his heel and headed to door. When he got there, however, he turned back around. Hand still on the push bar, he said, "Later, Raeby." He puckered his lips to blow a kiss as he left.

As the roar of his car engine faded down the street, Rae apologized to Natura. "I keep telling him to get lost. I can't wait to go back to CSU."

I gave Bert a summary before Natura got back to our table, but he still asked if everything was OK, as if he hadn't had the dragon eavesdrop on his behalf.

Natura brushed back her hair and took a swig of his beer before answering. "Carlton Quanz has been hassling Rae for a date since before I left. He and a couple of his buddies came here for lunch—slumming, I guess—and she turned him down then, but he keeps coming back. Taking advantage of my absence, I guess. Morrie even changed her shifts. His daddy may own the biggest pesticide company on the Front Range, but that kid is still a pest."

Bert chuckled. "Yeah, well, be careful swatting him. His Daddy already got him off one harassment charge."

She pursed her lips in disapproval. "I'm not surprised. That family thinks they can get away with anything. I heard they are looking into some kind of new fertilization process. Supposedly 'more natural.' It's, like, natural or it isn't, you know? There're no shades of gray here. My supplies are completely organic, no chemical fertilizers, no pesticides, no GMOs."

Was that why the food reminded me of home? I felt like there was something more to it, but my stomach was pleasantly full. I'd have to investigate further another time. I was ready for a nap.

Father seemed to be thinking along my lines. "Natura, the meal was amazing, as always, but I've got an early day tomorrow. Besides, we probably shouldn't overtax Beaver's generosity." He pointed to my anklet.

"Yes, about that! This was a gross violation of authority—of your rights, Vern. It is my solemn mission to free you. Tomorrow, I'll be contacting the Los Lagos Gazette and the Coloradoan, starting a petition on PetitIt.com..."

Bert held up his hands. "How about you give me twenty-four hours to talk to Beavers and the DA? You're right—there was no due process, so let's see if we can fix this under the system before we start bucking it?"

"'We'?" she said but nodded. "Fine. If Vern is amenable, we'll start with your way. But I will not rest until I see all our Faerie brethren treated with equality and respect. That's what brought me back to Los Lagos."

"Sure that wasn't your car breaking down?" Bert teased.

"No," she said in a tone that was half-teasing, half-exasperation. "And it wasn't the news; I have been completely off the grid since I started my walkabout. I was at Soulfire when I had a vision. The universe called me back. This must be why."

Back on the road, Bert smacked his hand on the steering wheel. "'The universe called me back.' Walkabout. What crap."

Father shrugged and looked out the window. "The journey of rediscovering oneself is a common element of every culture. But you know, it could be it wasn't the universe calling her back so much as the thought of one person in particular."

When Bert's only reply was a doubtful grunt, Father shifted to face him. "Bert, you're not fooling anyone. You've known her for over forty years. You took a dragon out of house arrest just to impress her. Now, make a move."

Chapter Nine: Dragon Plays D&D

I woke up with the taste of Natura's food still nagging at me. Yeah, I'm under house arrest, the one person who trusted me enough to give me a job is dead, Dona Elena still hasn't found her cat, and I'm thinking about last night's dinner. But there was something infuriatingly familiar about the taste that I just couldn't put my finger on—or tongue, as the case may be.

As Father and I sat down at the patio for breakfast, I mentioned it. "Any chance you could ask Natura to bring me over some samples?"

I heard Sister Bernadette cluck disapprovingly from the doorway and turned to see her carrying a huge bowl of eggs. Behind her, carrying a plate of toast and looking hesitant, was Teresa.

I held back a sigh. Guess this was going to be my business, after all.

“Where do think we’ll find the money to order you take-out?” Sister Bernadette asked as they set the food on the table. The bowl of scrambled eggs with ham seemed to testify to her statement. After I’d eaten two pounds of bacon in a single sitting, with Father consuming another half-pound “to keep me company,” she’d insisted bacon was thenceforth reserved for the day after fasting.

I chose to ignore her and greeted Teresa instead. “Not to be rude, but...?”

She ducked her head and poked at the eggs she’d spooned onto her plate.

Sister Bernadette answered as she served a heaping platterful for me. “She didn’t feel safe in the women’s shelter, so she’ll be staying with us for a day or two until we can find her better accommodations.”

Teresa glanced up at me, as if seeking permission, but it wasn’t mine to give. As long as she was here, though, there was no harm asking questions, right?

“Why don’t you tell us what happened that night?”

I got a scowl from Sister Bernadette, but Teresa took a sip of orange juice and answered. “I don’t know. Truly, I don't. We were in the fields. We were arguing. He grabbed me, then hit me. I couldn't stand it anymore. I shoved away and ran. I was yelling for help and praying. I didn't look back. I knew what would happen if he caught me. It was dark, and I wanted to get away. I heard him fall, and then... He screamed and screamed." She paused to shudder and rub her arms.

"Someone attack him, or some*thing*?" I asked and got kicked by a nun's shoe for my impertinence.

Teresa answered, her voice quiet with shame. "I didn't look back. I kept running. He was an athlete. He played football and was on wrestling team... I didn't want to know what could make him scream like that. But no one was around when he hit me. Could I have called an evil spirit to defend me?"

"Doubtful. But that doesn't mean something otherworldly hasn't taken up residence in that field. Bert needs to find a way to get me on that farm."

Father sighed. "I don't think that's going to happen. I think he pulled enough strings taking us to Natura's last night."

"Then I need more samples of her food—or at least to know where she gets her supplies."

Sister Bernadette shrugged and sipped her coffee before answering. "I don't know for certain, but don't her menus say she supports local farmers?"

Father's eyes widened, and he set his fork down. "How good is your sense of taste?"

"I can't taste ghosts, if that's what you're asking, but if it were magic... It could be what I'm sensing."

"What kind of magic would cause plants to strangle someone?" Sister Bernadette asked. "And what reason would anyone have for enchanting a field? Is this something that happens a lot in Faerie?"

"Not that I've ever heard of," I admitted, "but is murdering someone by choking them with plant matter a usual form of homicide in the Mundane?"

"Regardless, we should check it out," Father said.

"We?" his sister asked archly. "Are we back to the Nero/Archibald thing again?"

He ignored her. "If there's some kind of malignant magic and it's spreading... I'll talk to Bert. In the meantime, there's a Farmer's Market in town today. If we pick up some produce from the different farms, do you think you could tell if there's that same familiarness?"

I nodded, adding that I didn't sense anything dangerous in the food itself.

"It'd still be good to know if other farms are affected." He turned to Sister Bernadette. "It's our day off, Sis. The office is closed. Want to play hooky from that book you're writing and go to the Farmer's Market with me?"

"Go," Teresa said. "I'll be fine. I'll take care of dishes, then pray in the chapel until you return."

While they cleared the table, I went to the bookshelves to pick out something to read. I enjoyed their library. I'd been making my way through the theology section; it was interesting to see how closely the great theologians of both universes paralleled, and of course, some volumes found their way to Faerie regardless. The Faerie Catholic Church had always known about the Mundane world. We shared some of the same saints. More saints had the gift of bilocation than Mundanes knew about. Like George.

I looked down at my anklet. This is your fault, you know, George. If you hadn't taken away all my dragon greatness, I'd be in the Great Hibernation with my kin right now. God bless you, anyway, you pain in my tail.

I decided to skip the academics. Like Father said, it was our day off, and I enjoyed the incredible variety in Mundane fiction. I had to wonder if, as a result of being the only sapient species in their world, Mundanes had been forced to use their imaginations to fill a loneliness they didn't recognize they had. I poked my nose at the novels and pulled down a couple of mysteries. *The Killer Inside Me* spoke to the predator inside me. I snagged it along with *The Big Sleep* and *Altered Carbon*. That should last a lazy afternoon. I added a dictionary in case I came across any Mundane slang I couldn't decipher from the context.

Father and Sister headed out to the market, and I settled in the garden to read. The neighborhood was quiet, save for the occasional car, usually going faster than the posted speed limit, a lawn mower, and the squeak of Señora Dona

Elena's walker. Since she wasn't calling "Kitty" and I didn't smell an open tin of cat food, curiosity got the better of me, and I peeked around the church to see her hammering something to a lamp post. Hanging from her walker was a pouch with "Lost Cat" signs.

She finished her tapping, stuck the hammer in the pouch, and then set her walker on the street—just as a car was speeding up.

With a blare of the horn, the driver swerved, but not much. The breeze of his passing fluttered her hair and sent the handbills flying. Over her scream, I heard the boys in the convertible laughing. I took note of the color and make as well as the license place: GRW A PR.

"*Señora, ¿estás bien?*" I called out, but she was shaking her fist and swearing with such vehemence I thought she'd set her flyers on fire. Yeah, she was fine.

The Killer Inside Me gave me a whole new appreciation of the Mundane mind, both in its imagination and its capacity for viciousness. I told Father as much when he and Sister Bernadette arrived bearing small bags of fruits and vegetables.

Father grimaced at the title in my hands. "Yeah, we read that one in my undergrad psych class. Not a great representation of humanity, which is kind of the point. Good prep for hearing confessions though. Hard to be shocked after reading that."

We set aside the books, and they spread out the bags before me. Each contained produce from the farms in the local area, and using a map app on Sister's phone, we arranged them by distance from the McTaggert farm. I began my taste test with the produce from the farms nearest McTaggert's. Meanwhile, Father and Sister settled down with some sandwiches. It would have been the perfect picnic if we hadn't been using my taste buds to search out a killer.

"Not that one, either," I said after consuming the third offering. At least the variety was interesting, and they'd made sure to get chili peppers whenever possible since Jace was killed by chili pepper vines. I was enjoying the capsaicin. Since I couldn't breathe fire, the tingles the spice caused in my mouth were as close as I could get.

I heard the doorbell ring in the offices, and with a sigh, Sister Bernadette went to answer it.

"Well," Father said, "that's good news, anyway. We know that if it is magic, it hasn't spread somehow. Still, want to check out the rest? Just because the neighboring farms aren't contaminated doesn't mean this is an isolated incident, after all."

I'd ruled out the rest of the farms, much to Father's relief, when Sister Bernadette returned with several people in tow—the group from the comics store.

"Hey, are we interrupting a picnic?" Owen asked.

"Just a taste test," Father replied as he picked up the empty bags. He didn't elaborate; after all, we didn't have any authority to investigate a murder.

"Poblanos are my fave," Owen said, probably taking his cue from the chili pepper stenciled on one of the paper bags. "Not as hot, but they make the best rellenos. Anyway, we all have the day off, and thought we'd come check on you. We're really sorry about what happened. It's fracked."

"'Fracked'? Where'd you pick up dwarfish slang?"

"It's dwarfish?" He exchanged looks with his compatriots, and they said in unison, "Cool!"

Linda stepped forward. She had a large bag in her hands that bore a computer icon. "We know you wanted a computer, so we took up a collection at the comic book store, and..."

She set the bag down and pulled out a box with a computer on the label and a bunch of writing I didn't understand.

Father apparently did. He whistled in appreciation. "Maybe I should get tricked into house arrest."

Sister Bernadette smacked his arm then excused herself to go write. I assumed she wanted to check on Teresa, too. Our Damsel in Distress hadn't shown herself, and no one had mentioned her presence in front of the others.

Father suggested we take my gift to the garage.

"It's not the top of the line," Linda said in apology as a couple of the others unpacked it for me. "We were kind of limited by budget, but it does have some nice features. And we bought you an extra keyboard. We weren't sure about your claws, and this one's bigger and more easily replaced."

"Yeah, you can find them at thrift stores or on Amazon cheap," Owen said.

We spent the next half an hour loading software on the computer and showing me how it worked. It also twisted to work like a tablet, and they'd thoughtfully gotten me some rubber nibs that I could fit over my claws so I could use it without scratching the screen.

I've received a lot of tribute in my long life, from heifers to gems to priceless works of art, but few compared to this "cheap" computer purchased by a collection of strangers who didn't want anything from me and whom I hadn't threatened. It made up for a lot that had happened to me since crossing the Gap.

"So..." Ray started after he'd shown me how to email. "We were kind of wondering..."

Maybe my gratitude came too soon. "Yes?"

"It's just... This is usually gaming day for us, and we thought, if you didn't have anything to do, you might want to join our party?"

"We can roll you up a character," Owen added. "We're mid-campaign, but we'll roll you to third level and catch you up on the adventure. You're welcome, too, Father, I mean, if you're allowed."

Father laughed. "I'm going to get so much flak from Sister Bernadette. She used to tease me and my friends mercilessly about D&D when we were growing up."

"Wait—that nun is your sister?" Samwise asked.

"Yep, that's my sister the Sister, and I'm her brother the Father."

Father took the guys into the church to get a table and some chairs while Linda unloaded a cooler of sodas and bags of chips and other snacks from the car. As Samwise and Ray set up the table with a large map and arranged tiny models and figurines on it, Linda called a pizzeria and placed an order.

Sister Bernadette came out to see what the commotion was and declared us all "twelve" again. Father replied by sticking his tongue out at her, which made the humans laugh.

While Owen explained the NPC—that's a non-player character—that Father was taking over, I was given a handbook whose complexity and back-and-forth referencing reminded me of a grimoire. We rolled me up a character, a thief. I figured it added a nice irony to my week. Ray explained his role as DM to me and outlined the adventure, and then we were rolling dice and pretending to be completely different people in a completely different world.

Mundanes and their imaginations.

Sometime after we'd finished the pizzas, Captain Beavers dropped by.

"Now this is what I like to see," he said as he took in the nearly empty cooler, piles of pizza boxes and the half-dozen geeks, a priest and a dragon rolling dice and pushing around little figurines.

"Do you game?" Samwise asked.

"No," Beavers said with that good-natured laugh that nonetheless grated on my nerves. "I mean Vern making friends and staying out of trouble."

"Aw, we're a good influence," Samwise crooned, and the DM and I high-fived. I took the opportunity to pass him a note that I was going to pick Samwise's wizard's pocket for the ring of invisibility he wouldn't let me have after we looted the orcs we'd killed.

"Have you come to remove the anklet?" I asked Beavers. That would make today as close to a perfect day as I've had since coming to the Mundane universe.

Beavers twisted his face into a pained expression that said, "no." "Vern, Vern. We made an agreement. I'm sorry if you're finding it uncomfortable."

"Try unfair," Linda suggested.

Now, his eyes narrowed, and somehow, we'd just crossed a line. Nonetheless, he kept that good-friend smile plastered on his simpering face as he asked, "Could we speak in private, for just a minute?"

I passed Father my sheet and asked him to play my character, Pegjanu, and led the chief of police a little way toward the garden. When I thought we were well enough out of earshot, I stopped.

"You knew very well that I had no idea what this 'expensive jewelry' of yours was or what it meant," I said.

"You should have asked better questions," he countered. "And just because you didn't doesn't mean you are exempt from our agreement, even if you send the sheriff, the town social justice warrior, and your nerd friends to convince me or the DA otherwise. Legality is immaterial. I had to find a way to get you out of an assault charge. I didn't want to arrest you. Now, our hands are both tied."

"And yet, I'm the one chained to my 'house.' How long do you intend to keep up this facade of fairness?"

He spread his hands. "That depends entirely on you and how well you show you understand your place."

Dragons should not sputter. "My 'place'? My place was at the top of the food chain, of society, of the hierarchy of sapient beings. My place was one commanding respect—deference, even. My place..."

I stopped myself. That place hadn't been mine since St. George. For the past eight centuries, my place had been at the side of sapients, serving them under the direction of the Faerie Catholic Church. Then I got a calling to come here, and the Faerie Pope granted me leave to discover what God intended for me. Which, near as I could tell, was humiliation and trials to test even an elf's patience, let alone a dragon's.

I took a breath. "All right, Beavers. What *is* my place, in your opinion?"

"Well, now, I..." he stammered.

That's what I thought, but I pressed on. "Because I'm not allowed to make a home in the way of my species. My 'place' is not in the city plaza, if the protestors have anything to say about it, and judging by your reaction, they do. And now, I'm not allowed to leave the parish property. I don't think my place is sitting in a garage playing Dungeons and Dragons with a bunch of post-adolescent humans, fun as it may be."

"You need to learn to adapt..."

"Beavers, I have adapted to ice ages and primeval forests. I have lived among cultures your people have only dreamed about. I have played by the rules of peace and war of a dozen species. I adapted to being the size of a newt and posing as the pope's pet. But never have I been made so unwelcome and uncomfortable as I have among you Mundanes. So, I ask again, what is my 'place,' and how will we know I've found it so you can remove the Bracelet of Barriers?"

Once again, he gave me that patented pained look, but there was something else behind it—fear. And not of me.

I held up my leg. "Was it really your idea to restrict my movements?"

"Look, your friends are concerned and making a big noise about it, especially that Natura. That's not good for either of us. I just came by to explain that. I'm sure this will all blow over soon. Just be patient," he said.

He left without answering my question.

I may have been willing to be patient a little longer, but my new human friends were not.

"That blows!" Samwise said, and Owen and Linda agreed. After the party broke up, they'd hung around to show me more on the computer, including how to order food online. Of course, we were all hungry again, so they offered to demonstrate. I got take-out from Natura's, after all!

Or, more to the point, *delivery*. The idea of restaurants hand-carrying food to patrons in their own homes is uniquely Mundane and one I could get used to. I wished the Church would let me access my treasure. Maybe if I promised to tip the delivery people well?

In this case, Natura herself delivered the goods. She'd been planning to come by anyway, she said. She was feeling quite proud of herself for confronting Beavers until I had told her (and my new friends) the results.

"It totally blows," she agreed. "I thought I could appeal to him in the spirit of solidarity with the growing diversity of our world, but he's just a typical pawn of the system. Fine. That's groovy. We'll take this to the next level."

"I don't think Bert would appreciate another protest," I said, remembering our conversation of the night before. "For that matter, that's how I got in this trouble in the first place."

She held up her hands. "I dig, Vern. I really do. There's one more thing we can do in the system, and I know the person to help us. We do hot yoga together, so I know we'll be totally in sync. So, like, I hate to be a downer, but you should probably just lay low for now."

I twisted my head toward my new computer and my new friends. "I think I have enough to keep me entertained for a while."

As she left, I asked, "Natura, where do you get your produce?"

Caught off guard, she gave me a smile and answered easily. "McTaggert Farms—totally organic, environmentally responsible, and he pays his workers fair wages, no matter where they come from, so he's socially woke, too."

I had to look up "woke" later, but one thing I knew. Organic or not, there was a foreign—or should I say Faerie—element in his crops, and it was anything but responsible.

Chapter Ten: Lawyer Up

That Tuesday turned out to be the highlight of my week. After Owen, Samwise, and Linda left, the rest of the week pretty much settled into a routine of get up, pray, eat, read, do things on the computer, eat, pray, sleep. Oh, and let's not forget the time I spent hooked up to an outlet charging my "wonderful, state-of-the-art tech jewelry." I did it while I played on the computer, but it was still a drag, as Natura would say. I looked up dragons, and after weeding out the D&D references and something about "dragons loving tacos," I came up with the folklore.

Mundanes don't understand dragons at all. No wonder I was getting treated this way.

Natura called me on my computer (which, incidentally, gives better reception than a crystal ball) during a break in her hot yoga class to introduce me to "our" lawyer, Scott Youngman, Esq. Youngman wore tight leggings and a towel around his neck and kept bending himself into weird poses as he talked.

"I'm completely behind your cause," he said to me as he clasped one leg by the ankle and brought it to his ear. "It's clear-cut injustice, a heinous violation of your rights. The problem is, I'm completely consumed by discovery for another case I'm in, very high-profile, significant stuff."

More significant than me? Good thing I was amused by how easily he managed to snug his foot behind his neck. Maybe all the sweating helped.

"Yes," he said, though I hadn't asked any questions. "Very high profile. I'm representing the Safe Fuels Commission against the Los Lagos Nuclear Power Research Center for their role in creating the Gap. Undeniable negligence. Greater precautions should have been taken."

I didn't reply. He only knew half the story, it seemed. As the Mundanes were starting up their initial tests of the power plant, the Duke of Peebles-on-Tweed was ordering his wizards to open a portal from Faerie England to what Mundanes call "Georgia," but which is part of the Aztec Empire in my universe. Mages have been opening portals around our world for centuries, but usually, they have a contact on the other side or first-hand knowledge of the place. Duke Galen, however, was an impatient man and allowed himself to be reassured by mages that "having read about cantaloupes in a book" was sufficient for directing a spell.

Any other time, they might have landed someplace else—say, the garden of the Tavendor kingdom, and the Duke would have run through and swiped whatever melon was handy, victorious and none the wiser. But no. The spell touched upon the energy generated by the power plant, which was just charging up. That fed the spell and ripped a hole in our universes, forever tying them together. All this because the Duke Galen thought a couple of cantaloupes would make the Duchess laugh.

I decided not to mention this to Hot Yogaman. I did not think Bishop Aiden would appreciate me implicating his brother, the Duke, in a lawsuit, and I had no doubt my bendy lawyer could stoop that low. Besides, he'd returned his leg to its original position and had folded himself in half, holding one finger up to the screen in a "just a moment" signal.

"Much better," he said as he returned his torso to the upright position, then continued his conversation as if he'd not just treated me to a view of the small of his back. "Of course, they're claiming that all their records were destroyed in the explosion that caused the Gap, so everything's taking more time than anticipated. I barely have time for hot yoga and my weekly cleanse, but I can't do what I do if I don't take care of Number One, right?

"However, that's no excuse for not taking care of you," he said. "My office will be filing a 42 U.S.C. § 1983 action against the police chief and the city's police department. That should take care of it. They don't have a leg to stand on."

As if to emphasize his point, he pressed his right foot on his left knee and positioned his hands together as if in prayer.

After he hung up, I used my computer to look up "cleanse," and came up with a myriad of articles suggesting diets to help humans...poop? I read a couple of articles just to be sure I understood. I had read correctly, but I did not understand. Once again, I was impressed by the bizarre ingenuity of the Modern Mundane.

Still, some of the articles said it helped overcome alcoholism. I guess it wasn't enough for Rip Cliffman. Father had shown me a newspaper article; they'd recorded blood alcohol levels of .37 percent. Even accounting for potential errors caused by taking readings from a corpse, it was well above the legal limit at the time of death, the coroner had said. Natura steadfastly refused to believe it.

Father's week wasn't going much better. He had told Bert that I suspected magic in the fields, but Bert replied that we needed to back off and let the police do their jobs. Then, a couple of the migrant workers came to ask Father to bless the lands again, as they were going to be ploughing the fields under in preparation for winter. He took the opportunity to warn McTaggert that his land might be magically "contaminated." McTaggert flat-out told him to stop filling people's heads with superstitious nonsense.

"I have a dragon living in my garage, and he thinks magic is superstitious nonsense," Father complained over dinner that night.

"How do you think I feel?" I said. I was already frustrated that evening. At the behest of my friends, I'd joined one of their chat rooms and introduced myself. Despite the gaming group's assurances, everyone thought it was a gag.

"And no one is going to believe otherwise until you can make yourself known," Father said, loading his plate with another chili relleno. He'd gotten some peppers and a recipe from a worker at the McTaggert Farm. It definitely had the same familiar taint as Natura's food. "Maybe that's your Calling. To forge the way for other Faerie creatures."

"If so, I'm doing a poor job of it," I grumbled, looking at my anklet and the pile of leftovers Sister Bernadette had scraped onto my plate. I needed at least 30 pounds of food a day. Up until now, I'd been supplementing my diet with the local vermin. Not my first choice, but Sister was right—they could not afford to feed me. However, the local pests had learned to stay away from the parish land, and as long I had to wear that anklet, I could not venture further in the search for food.

If things didn't change soon, fasting would become my way of life—without the promise of bacon afterward. Too much fasting, and I'd be forced to eat kittens, lest my hunger drive me to larger, more sapient alternatives.

I didn't feel especially sanguine about changes coming soon.

Youngman's office filed the 42 U.S.C. and the next day, I got an email from Beavers: I thought we had come to an understanding. I'm very disappointed. I'd hoped we could be friends.

The next day, the DA filed a "Motion to Dismiss pursuant to Rule 12(b)(6)." The DA was arguing that the laws didn't apply since I was not a "person."

"Judge Simmons has decided he wants a hearing," Flexy Lawyerman told me over Xinga that afternoon. He was again at class with Natura, but this time, they were both in the picture, seated cross-legged facing each other and clasping each other's elbows. He had his neck craned back, so he spoke to the ceiling instead of to me.

"This really couldn't come at a worse time for me," he said, then paused as he and Natura shifted and raised their legs in an A between them, their feet pressed against each other's. "I'm going to have to completely revise my schedule, but what kind of lawyer—what kind of man—would I be if I let this challenge to the forward-thinking of our society go unanswered?"

"You're not alone in this," Natura said as they carefully switched their grips for a different stretch. "I'm already collecting character witnesses and doing the research. You're in capable hands, Vern. Namaste!"

She let go of Youngman to turn off her phone. I had to admire her balance. I also wondered if in court, he'd be cross-examining witnesses from the Cow Face Pose or the Half Lord of the Fishes Pose.

Tuesday rolled around to make its appearance again, and with it, my gaming buddies. They did not bear gifts of technology this time, so we got started on the campaign early, and Father wandered in just before lunch to play a little and avail himself of the pizza that was delivered—something Sister Bernadette had restricted because she thought he was getting a little paunchy.

"You know," he said ruefully as he grabbed his third slice, "I thought being a lifelong bachelor, I would have more say in my own diet."

Samwise sighed, "Maybe I should become a priest. Can they have dogs?" He reached down to scratch between Thunderpaws's ears.

"If you have to ask that, maybe you should learn a little more about the vocation before you consider it," Father replied.

"Don't mind him," Linda said. "We saw Rae arm-in-arm with that Carlton Quanz."

"I thought she'd told him off." Wow. I was curious about the love life of a human I'd never met. I really had sunk low. I blamed my captivity—and St. George, but that was reflex nowadays.

"Yeah, well..." Samwise sighed. "She's changed her mind. Guess he gave her a trinket and a sob story, and they've been connected at the hips ever since."

"Ew!" Linda said. "Not inaccurate, but still, ew!"

"Focus, people," Ray, our DM chided. "You come to a short side tunnel. Though dimly lit, you have the impression it opens into a wider cavern. You feel warmth emanating from it and the sound of deep, heavy breathing."

"It's the black dragon," Samwise hissed, *sotto voce*. "Maybe he's asleep. If so, Bandour, I can buff your Akaviri katana and you can get a surprise attack."

"Should we check first?" Linda asked. "I say we send in the thief."

All eyes turned to me and I shrugged. "Sure, I'll go sneak up on the huge, halfling-eating beast with nasty teeth and a nastier temper. What can go wrong?"

"Hold on!" Samwise whispered, "I'll lend you my ring of invisibility."

"You search your pockets and come up empty," the DM declared.

"What? But I had it. I haven't taken it out, and we haven't done anything that would make me drop it. Where's my ring?"

I held up one paw as if I had a ring pinched between my claws. "You mean this one? I slip it on and shuffle to the left."

"Pegjanu!" Samwise yelled my character's name, and everyone started laughing....

"And your outburst awakens the dragon. Roll for initiative."

And among the outraged howls and rolling of dice, who should appear but my lawyer. I almost didn't recognize him because he was wearing a suit instead of a leotard.

"Am I interrupting?" he asked.

"Yes!" my gaming friends chorused. Even Thunderpaws gave a yip of assent.

I waved my tail to invite him in. "Everyone, meet my lawyer, Hot Yogaman."

He laughed. "Scott Youngman, Esquire."

"Esquire," I added a half beat later.

Everyone shook hands, including Linda who blushed and called him hot before wincing and correcting herself.

"Do you need some privacy?" Father asked Scott.

"That's up to Vern, of course, but what I have is good news." At my go-ahead, he pulled some papers out of his briefcase. "It turns out, neither the judge nor the DA are especially interested in the media circus this hearing could grow into, so the DA has agreed to have Captain Beavers remove the anklet if you agree to drop the claim."

Cheers erupted all around. Youngman, Esquire, explained the release form while Father got me an inkwell. My pinkie claw is filed to handle ink like a quill. I have excellent penmanship, and

I allowed myself a moment of pride as everyone ooh'd and aah'd over my signature.

"I'll drop these off with the DA, and someone will be over to free you by the end of the day." As he picked up the form, he saw Linda's character sheet beneath it. "Oh, you have the Enchanted Broadsword of Elspeth. You should consider getting it silver-plated. It's plus-five damage to undead and, if you call on Elspeth, it glows once a day for five turns."

My compatriots watched him leave, Linda with a slight flush to her cheeks, the guys with a look that suggested they were rethinking their life choices. In the parking lot, he pointed his fob at a car that was wide, flat, and yellow. Its slanty headlights seemed to sneer superiority, and it bore a black crest with a gold bull and the word Lamborghini. It opened its doors at his command, and when he started it, it gave a growl that made me homesick for my kin.

Linda sighed. "I want to have his half-elf babies."

I said, "He's not an elf."

"Quiet. Momma's fantasizing." She rolled her dice. Nat20. "Oh, yeah.... Mmm! Okay. I'm good. Where were we?"

Soon, we were deep into battle. Linda's fighter had one hit point left and I was rushing to her side with healing potion while the Father kept the dragon distracted with magic attacks (a tactic which seldom worked, I can tell you, but no one asked). Samwise was about to confirm a critical hit when Father's phone went off.

Sam flubbed the roll. "Oh, come on!"

Father apologized before answering. "Bert? Hi, did you hear about Vern? He... What? Oh, no. It's good news for Teresa, sure, but... Do you need me? How about...? No, sure, I get it. Thanks for letting me know."

With my dragon hearing, I had picked up Bert's side of the conversation. "Another murder at McTaggert's farm?"

Father scowled at me reprovingly for my eavesdropping but nodded. "A hired hand went out early to plow the field under. Someone pulled him out and under the tractor while it was still running. However, this does mean Teresa isn't guilty. That's a relief, at any rate."

When he left, Ray said, "Someone or some-*thing*. I teach science at Zebulon Elementary. I have a lot of the migrant kids in my fifth-grade class. We were supposed to be dissecting flowers, but they refused. They said *Las Viñas* would kill them in revenge."

"Could they be right? I mean, could the plants be enchanted for real?" Linda asked.

I shrugged. "If so, it's not any spell I've heard of, but McTaggert won't let me on the land to check it out."

"Small-minded man," Linda said. "Could you do something if it is an enchantment?"

"Personally, no, but I could sense it enough to tell you if you need a wizard, a creatures-keeper, or an exorcist."

"We should go check it out," Samwise declared. "At night, when no one's around. My uncle's farm is right next door. We can sneak in from there. I mean, what if it is something otherworldly, and it decides to move? My uncle could be next."

It was decided. After my anklet came off, they'd come get me, supposedly to celebrate. We'd go to his uncle's farm and if I couldn't sense the magic from the fence line, we'd sneak in just until I could get a sense of what-if-anything was causing the fields to develop a taste for human blood.

Before dinner, everyone left with the promise to return around 10:30—conveniently after Father's bedtime—to "celebrate," but apparently, either Flexy Lawyerman was stretching his estimate of the DA's ability to do speedy paperwork, or Beavers wasn't as keen to let me go so easily. The new estimate was noon tomorrow.

"We got all prepped," Samwise whined. And they had. Camo and chainmail made an interesting fashion mix, and they wore the same kind of boots I'd seen on the military who formed the Mundane's first Welcome Crew.

"Can you tell us what to look for?" Linda asked.

I shook my head. If I could, I'd have told Father or Bert. "Humans don't have the ability to sense or manipulate magic. You need Magical blood for that."

"Anyone know how to hack the anklet?" Ray asked, then said, "What? They admitted this was bogus, and they were supposed to have removed it today. Why should Vern have to suffer? Besides, there have already been two deaths. What if McTaggert decides to send more people to plow the field—or burn it?"

I considered his words. "What exactly does this thing detect?"

"Just location, why?"

I unhinged a couple of joints and slid the anklet off. My lawyer had told me to be patient. Instead, I decided to follow his example and be flexible.

Chapter Eleven: Commandos, Cars, and the Crazy Cat Lady

Despite the dark, I rode in the back of Samwise's truck under a tarp. It would have been an ignoble journey, except for the fact that Linda and Owen joined me...

No, I take that back. It was ignoble. They never stopped giggling about going on a real adventure with a real dragon.

After we left the road and endured a series of spine-jarring bounces, we came to a stop. We pushed the tarp off and breathed in the crisp air.

"Well?" Owen asked.

I shook myself from snout to tail and flapped my wings with a firm snap to release the kinks before folding them. "We'll need to get closer."

"Yes!" Owen pulled out his sword and buckled it on.

His companions snickered.

He shrugged. "Hey, this is my tournament sword. I cut bamboo with it. It is razor sharp."

A few minutes of trudging brought us to the edge of the chili fields, and I did sense something. Definitely Faerie. Definitely magic. But distant and...sad? Spells didn't have emotions.

I lowered my head to the ground and sniffed at the nearest vine. Capsaicin, small animal scat, the exhaust so prevalent in the Mundane, human blood—but no magical creatures that I could smell. But I got a sense of magic and of grief. I let my companions know.

"Maybe whatever killed the farmhand regrets it?" Linda asked.

If so, it might be hiding. "Wait here."

I took a careful step into the field, then another, and another, each as unmolested as the first. After I'd gone about five paces without villainous vines rising to strangle me, I heard footsteps as first Owen, then Ray, then Linda, Samwise and even Thunderpaws followed.

"Stay between the rows," Owen suggested.

Since I didn't know where the first victim was killed—and wasn't too interested; it was days ago, and it sounded like he deserved it—I led us to the tractor.

"Guys," Sam asked, shining his flashlight on a blood-coated leaf. "Is that what I think it is?"

There were grunts of agreement. Even Thunderpaws whined.

"It's old," I reassured him. "Just don't make any aggressive moves."

Linda had directed her flashlight toward the tractor. "Look at that!"

The vines had tangled in the wheels and the blades and crawled up the side into the interior, as if the tractor had been there for years rather than hours. Owen said someone leaked on the Internet that the driver had been dragged under and through the tilling blades, and then his mutilated body was flung astride the back of the tractor.

"I'm going to be sick," Samwise muttered but approached the tractor anyway.

"Could the plants be alive?" Linda asked. "I mean, of course they're alive, but I mean alive, like sentient?"

Ray nudged a plant with his foot. "Maybe we should take one with us to study." And before I could voice a protest, he had pulled it out by its roots.

The sadness around me exploded into rage.

"Drop it!" I ordered. "Drop it and run."

"Guys!" Samwise whimpered. Vines had wrapped around his ankles.

Owen yanked out his sword and chopped at the vines. *Las Viñas* surged around us, grasping for our arms and legs. Mixed with the rage, I felt waves of general frustration and very targeted spite. This vengeful vegetation intended to teach the humans a lesson, starting with the meddling kids and their dragon companion.

For flora, these chili pepper plants were surprisingly articulate. Could they be sentient?

I hopped onto the hood of the tractor where I'd have room to move. With a combination of hiss, wing flaps, and tail swishes, I spoke in Nymph Common. "Calm down. We're trying to help you."

Meanwhile, my "brave" companions shrieked like pixies and tore across the field, trying to stay between the rows, keeping their limbs tucked in close yet still batting at a stray vine. Ray had taken the lead, Linda close behind, calling for Thunderpaws to follow. The valiant little corgi, however, was dancing around Samwise, yipping and pulling at the vines that had again snagged his master. Owen doubled back to hack him free. Naturally, that made him the prime target once again.

I leapt from the tractor and landed near him, snapping at the vines slithering toward Owen's feet. They reared back, but while my head was occupied protecting his ankles, an attack was being waged against my own limbs, and having seven (four legs, two wings, and a tail) I was hard pressed to stay clear. I tried again to explain in Nymph Common that we were trying to help, but the creepers had pulled on my left wing and tail, effectively muting me.

Halfway down the field, Linda screamed and fell, tripped by the pepper plants.

So much for being a nice drake. I launched myself into the air, ripping plants from the ground. I swear, I felt them scream. They loosened and fell off me. I turned towards Linda. She was already half covered.

"Owen!" I called, and with a cry of acknowledgement, he abandoned Samwise to help Linda. I roared a warning any creature of Faerie would understand, but the vindictive vegetation did not react. I swooped down, grabbing Sam with my claws and Thunderpaws with my tail. With a surge of my wings and some magic of my own, I lifted them both. We skimmed over the field, an occasional vine reaching up to take a swing at us. I dropped the two off at the tree line, ricocheted off the trunk of a sturdy oak, and flung myself back toward the others.

Owen had managed to free Linda and was pulling her up. I told Owen to run and took care of Linda myself. She was gasping and shaking under my grip, but otherwise all right. I deposited her at the tree line, and she nearly fell into Ray's and Sam's arms, but after a moment pushed back, insisting she was fine. As soon as Owen stepped out of the danger area, she threw her arms around him.

"You saved my life!" She sobbed against his shoulder for a minute, while the others panted and shook off the last of the broken plant matter.

Then, they all started laughing.

"That was so amazing!" Linda squealed.

"I can't believe we just battled enchanted vines!" Samwise added.

"Did you get it all on the GoPro?" Owen asked.

We headed back to the car, the lot of them scraped and bruised, their clothes smeared with dirt and chlorophyll, chatting about how everyone was going to freak with envy that they, the Guardians of the Gap, had gone on an actual live adventure with a real dragon.

I sighed. Mundanes.

On the way home, I rode alone under the tarp while everyone else crowded into the cab to discuss our options. Linda lent me her phone so I could participate. In the end, we decided that they should drop me off before going home and calling in an anonymous tip. There was a heated debate about whether anyone would accept an anonymous tip that went, "I was trespassing in the field, and when I pulled up a root, the vines came to life and attacked me," but given what Bert had already seen and the botanical carnage we'd inflicted, it seemed like the best shot. If worse came to worse, they'd edit the video to obscure their faces and send it to Bert.

They dropped me off at the edge of the parish grounds, and I let myself in the back door of the garage. The anklet waited in the charger, emitting a languid red glow, uncaring at having been left alone all evening. I slipped it on, then settled down into a sleep haunted by dreams of leshies ticking me to death with their beards while nymphs whipped me with their hair and yelled that it was all my fault.

I woke up after only a few hours' sleep, itchy under my scales and smelling like spicy weeds. I used the garden hose to wash off before Beavers' men came to free me. The last thing I needed was to clue them in that I'd been off property. Even if Beavers didn't think I'd been trespassing, he'd surely use it as an excuse to keep the anklet on.

The early morning air was chilly, especially with damp scales, so I circled the church grounds looking for the best spot of sunshine in which to dry off. As I rounded the corner to the street side, I caught sight of Dona Elena hobbling toward a cat in the middle of the road, sweetly cooing to it in Spanish and completely unaware of the car speeding straight toward her.

"*¡Cuidado!*" I shouted to get her attention as I bounded toward her. I ploughed into her, half lifting her and half-tripping over her walker as I let momentum carry us to the other side of the street. We tumbled onto the grass as the car sped by. Dona Elena screamed, as did the woman in the convertible. The driver, however, laughed as he sped on over the protests of his passenger.

"*Señora, ¿estás bien?*" I asked. Behind me, I heard a car screech to a stop and the anemic slam of a car door.

I backed off as Dona Elena struggled to sit up, crying "*La gatita! La gatita!*"

Figured. It was all about the cats with this one. I brought round the puffed-out, angry, hissing little ball of trouble and dropped it into her waiting arms. She shrieked in pain as it dug its claws into her chest and escaped over her shoulder.

There was a loud *Pop!* and something poked me in the side.

I plucked out the dart that had struck me just below my back scales. Then I realized Fischer from the Department of Immigrations was standing at his car, loading his rifle with another.

"Back away slowly, ma'am. I'll protect you," he said as he aimed again.

"You have got to be kidding me," I moaned. Already, I felt light-headed. What was that stuff?

"I was saving her life," I said, though already my words were getting bleary and I may have spoken Faerie common.

Dona Elena added her protests to mine. Maybe he didn't understand Spanish. Maybe he didn't care.

Another dart pierced my side.

"Stop that!" I said, though I didn't make a move toward him. My legs were starting to feel like lead, and a dark spot was growing between my eyes.

That's when I realized I was on the wrong side of the street. I'd broken my parole. Beavers was sure to use that against me. I tried to drag myself back to the church and got another dart for my efforts.

At this point, Dona Elena decided to take things into her own hands. Screaming obscenities, she rushed—yes, rushed—forward, grabbing a broken piece of her walker. She slammed it on Fischer's knuckles, making him drop the gun, then continued to whack him, all the time screaming that he was a terrible dogcatcher and should have been trying to find her cat instead of picking on innocent dragons. I was touched and vowed to tell her so after the world got back into focus.

The last thing I saw clearly was Dona Elena suddenly drop her club and buckle over. I tried to cry out to her, but blackness fell over me like a thick blanket.

When I came to, the first words out of my mouth were the ones I'd intended to say before I lost consciousness: "Help her, you idiot!"

The second words I spoke made more sense to my new situation. "Great. What lunacy have they thought up for me now?"

I'd awakened under a broad-leafed tree that cast dappled shadows upon my scales. I rested on clean sand. Somewhere behind me, a small waterfall was making a happy sound as its water tumbled over boulders.

It would have been downright peaceful if it wasn't sitting on cement and encased in glass and a mesh ceiling.

The Mundanes had tossed me in the zoo.

Head pounding and groggy, I took in my surroundings. I was apparently in the inclement weather part of the exhibit; a barred door cut me off from the waterfall and large roaming area. A glass wall separated me from the squarish interior where humans came to gawk at the animals. Right now, I was the one being gawked at. On one side of the square, primates clung to tree branches and showed me their teeth. On another side, large cats watched me with wary eyes. Even though barriers they thought were unbreakable separated us, I could sense their fear. Except for the sloths on the third wall of cages. They didn't seem to care.

Inside was eerily silent, yet outside the building, humans were chanting for my freedom, while others were shouting, "Send the monster back."

Inside the building, the only human was a priest bent over his rosary.

I hauled myself to my feet and tapped on the glass. "All right, Father. I'm awake. You want to explain what's going on?"

"Explain?" Father exploded back at me, sparking pandemonium. Monkeys screeched, tigers roared and threw themselves at the glass. Father outyelled them all. "Why don't you explain, Vern? How could you attack Dona Elena?"

"What?"

Father opened his mouth to speak again just as a chorus of chimps decided to add their voices to the fray. I roared—a true dragon's roar, the roar of a predator on his last nerve and ready to use them all as stress snacks. Everyone went quiet—chimps, primates, wild cats... Even the protestors paused.

"I didn't attack anyone," I said into the silence.

"She's in the hospital, Vern! Bruises and cuts... She had a heart attack."

"And she said I attacked her?" Maybe she had a stroke, too, because her brain was addled.

"She hasn't said anything. She's still unconscious. The doctors don't think she'll make it."

"Oh." I sat down hard, my anger momentarily gone. Señora Dona Elena was a pain in the tail, but she'd had the spunk to confront me when everyone else was running to Father or hiding behind the law or protest signs.

Father slumped against the glass, his anger spent.

I murmured a Faerie prayer for her healing, then explained about the cat, the car, and Fischer. I kept my voice calm, but loud enough to be heard through the thick glass. Father sat on the sill of the window, with his ear against the pane. Someone—well, someone Catholic from Faerie—seeing his posture might think he was hearing my confession, although the only thing I was confessing was my innocence.

"All the bruises and cuts on Fischer?"

"Her doing, not mine. She's got a nasty swing. I was too woozy on tranquilizers to move. You Mundanes make some strong potions."

"Let me call Captain Beavers. Maybe we can salvage this. And Vern, I'm sorry. I should have realized attacking people is not in your character."

As it turned out, Father's smartphone was too dumb to make a call from within the building, so he excused himself and left, ducking under the post barrier that kept people away from the glass. As he went in search of better reception, I was left to ponder the reception I'd received from the Mundanes. Not the happiest of thoughts when outside, people were pointing cameras into my cage, and the opposing protestors not only out-shouted my defenders but had changed their chant to "Euthanize him!"

"You can't kill a dragon, you stupid Mundanes," I hollered to the ceiling. "We're immortal beings!"

But they sure could make me wish I were dead.

I don't know why it took so long for Father to make a simple phone call.

The crowd had received the message about my unkillable nature and were now demanding my body parts be harvested and sold to the wizards to "pay for damages." So far, my damages consisted of a broken walker and a terrified cat. And a broken security anklet. I'd decided I was already incarcerated, so why continue to bear the insult? I didn't bother unhinging my joints. I used my teeth. More satisfying that way.

I blamed Dona Elena's coronary on Fischer, but I'd be willing to foot her bill, too. It'd probably cost an arm and a leg, but I'd grow them back eventually, and it'd be a small price to pay for freedom.

If I thought they'd stop there. Which I didn't.

I kept under the shade of the artificial tree and resisted the urge to fly up and heckle the press and the protestors. Bishop Aiden had made me promise to be patient with the Mundanes, and by George, I was going to put on a display of supreme patience before I decided to truly lose my temper.

Once upon a time, sapients would have paid dearly for inflicting less insult to me than these Mundanes had. When had I forgotten what—who—I was? How long had it been since I truly commanded the respect due my species instead of demanding it like some spoiled nobleman?

Maybe it was a good thing my kin were all in hibernation. I was an embarrassment to my species.

By the time Father returned with Beavers in tow, I had entered a different kind of determined rage. I was going to get the respect my kind deserved, or I was going to make people pay.

Perhaps Beavers sensed it; he remained on the other side of the post barrier. In the meantime, Father excused himself again and went back outside.

Beavers pulled out a little notebook. "Fischer reported that he drove up, saw you crouched over

Mrs. Costa, pinning her with your claws while strangling her cat. While he was grabbing his tranquilizer gun, you threw the cat in her face and turned on him. We only have one other witness, but she was in her house and never saw anything. She said she heard screams, screeching brakes, and gunshots, so she hid in the pantry. Now, Father said you saved Mrs. Costa from a speeding car? What evidence do you have?"

Placing Fischer above Beavers on my mental mauling list, I described the incident, the car, and its driver. "I'd seen it before, too. The driver had just missed her that time. I think he may have swerved toward her to make it close. The license plate was GRWAPR."

He made a note, but otherwise didn't react to the unusual plate. "Well, I'll do what I can. It's important to me that the streets of Los Lagos are safe for children to play in and old women to cross. Now, the real question is, what do we do about you?"

I had a whole list, but I stuck with an easy one. "Let me go and make sure everyone knows I'm innocent."

He laughed as if he honestly thought I was making a joke. "I'm afraid it's gone too far for that, Vern. You've frightened a lot of people. They're calling for your head."

That would be a long, painful recovery. "I thought you were supposed to protect and serve. Doesn't it say that on your cars?"

"But that's exactly what I'm going to do. If you just cooperate."

"Like I did when you tricked me into wearing that thing?"

"Where is..." He scanned my ankle, then saw the twisted piece of fabric and metal I'd abandoned by the tree. He *tsked.* "Oh, Vern. Vern, you're just making it worse."

Outside, the crowd's chants dissolved into chaos, and I heard new shouts: "Down with Catholics!" "The Faerie Church are invaders!" "Take your pet and go to hell!"

I jerked my head toward the chaos. "I'm making it worse? You have hostile humans loose in your town, hostile magic loose in your farms..."

Why did he give a start when I said that? I was too mad to care. "Your people are out of control and in danger, yet you are obsessively focused on me."

"That'll do, Vern," an authoritative voice with a slight brogue cut me off. "Matthew 5:39."

Bishop Aiden approached with Father Rich. He looked from the other cages to mine, and I reveled in the fury in his eyes. Finally! Someone who understood how wrong all this was.

He bowed slightly to me. "Vern, I owe you an apology. Had I realized how...utterly unprepared the Mundanes were to understand your significance, I would have counseled you to patiently remain on our side of the Gap. Moses was right to call Mundanes a 'stiff-necked people.' Apparently, they are blind as well. I ask your permission to make reparations."

Beavers cleared his throat. "Well, that's very kind of you, Bishop."

"I was speaking to Vern, not you." He gave the chief of police a haughty annoyed glance, then returned his gaze to me. "By your leave, Magnificent One?"

I didn't know how much of this was for show and how much of this was genuine kowtowing, but I allowed myself to be soothed. That's when I noticed I'd dug divots through the packed dirt and into the cement floor with my claws. I retracted them surreptitiously while distracting everyone by giving a regal nod and saying, "By all means, Your Excellency. Perhaps a human touch is needed."

Bishop Aiden may have a human touch, but that didn't mean he wasn't going to be heavy-handed. "By the authority of the Catholic Church of Faerie and the Duchy of Peebles-on-Tweed, upon which the Gap opens, I demand the immediate release of Vern, a citizen of Faerie and one of the most respected beings of our world."

Now, he was laying it on thick. I hadn't been "most respected" of anything since George. Not that I was going to correct him, of course.

Beavers spread his hands. "But, Bishop, that was our intention all along. Your trip was completely unnecessary—unless, of course, you'd like to attach his manacles yourself."

"*Manacles?*" I'm not even sure I said the word in English or in my own tongue. The animals again exploded into panic. Smart creatures. The last time I was in manacles was standing before

Satan's lieutenants, and it did not end well for them.

"Vern..." the Bishop warned, slipping into Faerie Common. "Calm, I pray thee."

"Calm? Did you hear what they were shouting earlier? These Mundanes want to dissect me and sell the pieces. Do the legends say what happened the last time a group of humans thought that was a good idea? Because I've forgotten the details, but it's coming back to me."

My mouth formed the words, but that was not the only part of me communicating. My cheek crests flared. My wings had unfurled. My claws were out, and I radiated danger. The wild cats had fled through their open doors and into their outdoor domain, where I'm sure they'd found hiding places as far from me as possible. All the primates had retreated to the farthest corners of their habitats and huddled together. Even the sloths had moved to the highest parts of their cages.

The humans, however, hadn't budged. Stupid meat that they were.

Father was wide-eyed and shaking. Bishop Aiden had seen my furies before; he knew not to back down, but also to not provoke me. He held up his hand as if to bless me.

Then Beavers said, "See? This is exactly the reason–"

I swiped at the glass with my claws, scraping six-inch lines an inch deep.

Beavers yelped and stumbled back.

I swung again, scoring more deeply, and was rewarded when he fumbled for his gun. Oh, yes, Meat. Come on! You really think a couple of ounces of lead is going to stop me?

I raised my claws to strike again.

Then suddenly, between me and my intended victim was a shimmering apparition in full plate mail, broadsword, and that billowy cape I always teased him about. St. George.

His eyes met mine, and he wagged a gloved finger at me.

I roared in frustration and catapulted myself into the air. I tore through the mesh ceiling like paper, causing the humans to scream, duck, and cower. I strafed some, yanking a protest sign from one's hands, then took to the air. Just like the Bishop instructed, I turned the other cheek, but I didn't give them the opportunity to shoot it with bullets or tranqs.

I flew at my best speed toward the Gap, but in the Mundane, information flies faster. As I cleared the farmlands and outskirts, I saw Bert's SUV, lights on, sirens blazing, and going all out on the highway below me. If he thought I was going to stop and talk, he was sorely mistaken.

Ahead of me lay the Gap, a large, roundish, perpetually open gateway between our universes. Humans saw a kind of dull brown weaving—like burlap, Bert had once told me. To a dragon, the Gap was a fantastic kaleidoscope of magical energies too complex for even my dragon mind to track. Right now, it was the most achingly beautiful thing I'd seen in months.

A line of military vehicles blocked my path. Men with rifles crouched behind them, weapons pointing to the sky.

Well, this was going to hurt. All of us.

But Burt's SUV cut the sirens and I heard his voice coming from the loudspeakers. "Stand down! Stand down! Let him through."

I saw a ripple of confusion, but by the time I'd reached the line, every weapon had been lowered.

I passed through the Gap unmolested. Fresh air devoid of exhaust and redolent with magic greeted me.

I was home.

Chapter Twelve: Dragon Goes Home

As was typical for early Fall in Peebles-on-Tweed, the sky was cold, dark, and threatening rain. I didn't care. I was passing through, anyway. I'd had it with Mundanes, the Catholic Churches of Faerie and Earth, and humans in general. In fact, if I didn't see a sapient for a hundred years, it would be too soon. I snagged myself a juicy sheep for a meal since there's no delivery where I was heading.

There are exactly 70 dragons in existence, and each had its own territory. I knew this, knew it with some instinct, but in the battle with St. George, my memories had become casualties. I could not remember my kind—no names, no faces, no scents. All I knew was that they had entered a Great Hibernation, but no one knew why or why I was left out of the call to sleep. I was alone in my world.

Yet some instinct told me that Peebles-on-Tweed was not my Territory, and if one of my kind caught me lounging in her stuff, there'd be trouble. I flew east and south, across the strait, over Faerie France, and on to what we call Medsea and the Mundanes call the Mediterranean, which is practically the same thing. Lots of parallels between Faerie humans and Mundanes. Too bad an instinctive respect for dragons wasn't among them.

Somewhere along the Iberian Peninsula, I felt a rightness come over me, and I knew I was on my turf. I forced myself not to think, but to let my wings and my heart lead the way to a high cliff overlooking the sea. Below, mermaids frolicked in the surf. When they saw me, they waved hands and fins and called for me to come play. I liked mermaids. Though sapient, they had the relative attention span of the fish they shared their sea with. This made them ditzy and playful, but I was not in the mood for company.

I soared into the cave for as far as I could keep my wings spread, then walked, following the warm scent of gold until I found it: a warren packed almost to the ceiling with ancient coins, precious stones and various artifacts. I gave a joyful shout that a lesser being might have mistaken for a sob and threw myself into the pile. I rolled and wiggled and enjoyed the soothing comfort of precious metals against my skin. This was a dragon bed!

A small carving loosed itself from my pile and rolled to the floor. The Miraculous Virgin. Clad in a white robe with a white mantle embroidered in gold, she looked like a statue I'd seen in Father Rich's church. Her face was uncannily lifelike, and she seemed to gaze at me with loving reproof.

Nope! I was not going to feel guilty. I wiggled myself deeper into my pile until I was completely covered with only my nostrils exposed for breathing and several cubic inches of beautiful, heavy, soothing gold between me and the disapproving gaze of the human Mother of God.

I'd just managed a few deep, relaxing breaths, when a familiar voice said, "Hiding in your hoard? I'm not sure if that's a typical dragon move or not."

"Go away," I said to the apparition of St. George. "You're dead."

"And you're more bull-headed than a minotaur. I know because I met one thanks to you. I was stuck in his foul-smelling caves for six months while he mocked me and made my life miserable before he finally agreed to show me the way out."

"Yeah," I said, chuckling at the memory. "Good times. Wait. Is this an object lesson?"

I pushed my head to free it from my bedding. Some of the coins flew through St. George's ghostly form. He continued to sit cross-legged in the air, sharpening his sword like he often did when we talked. The first few months of our friendship, I'd thought he had wanted it handy in case our arguments got heated. Later, I'd learned that he'd needed to keep his hands busy. Guess some things don't change, even in death: fidgety hands, the need to kick me when I'm down...

No, that wasn't fair. After our battle ended in a stalemate, he'd grown into a good friend. One of the few who had the guts to tell me when I was wrong.

Ah, fewmets. This was an object lesson.

"You dealt with one bull-headed Magical. There are eight billion stubborn Mundanes."

"They weren't all against you. That Owen has some impressive swordsmanship. You can tell him I said so."

"That's presumptuous. Who said I'm going back?" I regretted my words the moment I said them. We both knew Who. The real question was, how long was I going to put off a Divine Calling?

The Mundane Bible had the story of Jonah who was swallowed by a whale after fleeing God's call. In our Bible, we also had the story of the great whale Cetus, who refused God's command to eat King Sulemani's supplies to teach the king a lesson about hubris. Cetus really hated corn. He was forced to carry a human in his stomach until he relented.

But they knew their mission. They had a goal. Me, all I was given was a vague feeling of "Cross the Gap and figure it out."

I thought about asking George, but I couldn't make myself admit my ignorance. He probably wouldn't know. Besides, I was a dragon; I should be able to figure it out. So instead, I asked him if he had any advice for dealing with a bunch of bull-headed Mundanes.

"Same way I dealt with a bull-headed Faerie—more than one," he added, giving me a teasing nod. "Patience, perseverance, and prayer. I know it won't be easy. For six months I endured Asterion mocking me, fighting with me, and let's not forget the 'presents' he left in my path. It was dark and smelled of musk and dung, and all I had to eat was lichen. Oh, yes, that was a highlight. John the Baptist had honey to go with his locusts. The Jews had manna. Me, I had dirty green moss I had to scrape from the walls."

"Is that why you swore off broccoli?"

George pointed his sword at me, a warning to stay focused. "Toward the end, though, something happened. Asterion talked with me. We developed a grudging respect. I was able to bring him to our side—and you know better than I what a useful ally he became. My point is that there is a reason God Called you to the Mundane, and it's not because it's easy. You need to have more faith."

"Easy for you to say," I grumbled. "You're a saint."

"Now. But back then, I didn't know what I was meant to do. I had to make an act of faith. Otherwise, I would have just followed the markings I'd made and escaped the Minotaur's maze, and what would that have accomplished?"

"What markings?" I asked, but he'd already faded from sight.

"No one likes a smug saint!" I shouted into the emptiness.

Despite George's version of a pep talk, I was not in a hurry to return. For one, I wasn't even sure how I could accomplish that. Not only had I made a rather dramatic exit, but if I hadn't left, I would have been escorted to the Gap in chains. I didn't think swallowing my pride would be enough. I needed a solid reason for my return and a reason for the Mundanes to keep me. I'd need time to think about that.

Besides, it had been too long since I could actually be a dragon. I slept sprawled out on my back, my treasure supporting me, so my spikes didn't dig into my spine. I took long relaxing flights and frolicked with the mermaids. They begged my help against a shark that was terrorizing their waters, so I enjoyed sashimi for lunch before returning to the warm waters of Medsea for a second bath.

Finally, relaxed, sated, and clean, I retired to the shore and regaled the mesmerized merfolk with stories of Mundane technology. Word of my arrival had spread, and other sapients came to visit and learn. One High Elf, a scholar of languages, asked me about their written words, and I took great amusement in telling them about human texting and how they threw out all the rules of grammar in favor of brevity. I wrote some in the sand along with the translations while he gaped in shock. Considering the long-windedness of the High Elves, he'd probably puzzle over this for years.

I was puzzling, too. Cliffman had sent Father two meticulously precise texts, and Natura had said that wasn't normal for someone who was intoxicated. I didn't like my explanation that someone had swiped his phone and texted in his place. First, why bother? It didn't accomplish anything, and it wasn't funny. Second, I'd carefully watched my human friends, and it didn't occur to any of them to use proper punctuation. Of course, Rip's hadn't been grammatically perfect, either.

Idly, I started to scribble Cliffman's apologies into the sand.

"Is that poetry?" the elf scholar asked, though, in the native language of his people, that simple sentence took him 10 minutes to say.

In the meantime, I contemplated the content of Cliffman's text as if for the first time.

Vern,
Again, apologies.
Very sorry.
Everyone isn't against you.
Never give up!
Get out there and solve this.
Even with these setbacks, you can do it.
My faith in you is strong.
Everything will work out.

Vern, Avenge Me? Great. What did that mean? The other message, "My apologies. You Are not to blame. Don't give up on us mundanes. Everything will work out in the end. Rip," spelled MYADER.

Or did it? I scratched out "you are" and replaced it with text abbreviation: UR.

MURDER

Well, there goes my vacation. I could hardly deny that I had no reason to return to the

Mundane. The handwriting was on the wall. Well, in a text, but the message was the same.

I took the standard hour and a half to say a proper Elvish apology to my visitor, which he graciously accepted. He wasn't too upset. The mermaids had called for him to talk to them, and even the famous focus of the High Elves was no match for a watery maiden wearing C-cup seashells.

Of course, there was the question of getting past the military that guarded the Mundane side of the Gap. I'd given it some thought while I was among my treasure, and so before I left, I snagged one of the rings to take with me. Then I flew west to the nearest monastery for Our Lady of Miracles and explained my situation to the mages there. Fortunately for me, they were only too glad to help me return to my Calling. One of the nuns empowered my ring with an invisibility spell. I thought my D&D friends would appreciate the irony.

After the disaster that created the Gap, the mages of the world agreed to restrict portal travel to well-known routes only. We were lucky connecting to the Mundane world, my current situation excepted. No one wanted to risk opening a second rift into a more hostile environment. Thus, the closest they could get me to Peebles-on-Tweed was one of their sister monasteries on the shores of France. (Yes, we have a Faerie France. Great food; uptight chefs. They once had an entire war over desserts.)

Still, the portal saved me about 10 hours of flying, and even after being pressed to judge between Brother Andre's *joyeuse confiture de raisin* and Brother Jean's *marmelade d'orange miséricordieuse*, I'd cut a lot of time off my trip.

I flew the rest of the way under clear skies and with a nice tail wind, which gave me the opportunity to think. Why would someone want to kill Rip, and why would he try to tell me in particular? True, he'd sent Father the texts, but he addressed me both times.

He knew someone was after him, probably watching him. That's why he'd coded the message. But the murderer could not have been too close, or he would not have let him send the text at all. If he knew someone planned to kill him, why not go to the police?

I snorted. Right–go to Captain "No Problems Here" Beavers. I was liking him less and less.

Still, Bert's trustworthy. Or there was the state patrol. Why go to me? Not that humans hadn't asked me to be the agent of vengeance before, mind you, but Mundanes didn't know that. No, there had to be something specific he thought I could help with.

I ran through our brief acquaintance. He gave me a job. Was there something wrong at the plaza or maybe the museum? With Barry Mann? I chuckled at that thought. I could see the trigger-happy guard accidentally killing someone, but Barely Man was too incompetent and lazy to be a murderer.

The pickpocket that bumped into him and I later captured had been released by Beavers. Would he have had time to arrange Cliffman's death before catching a bus out of town? Rip died by driving off a mountainside while drunk. Was he being chased? If so, that lets the pickpocket out.

He had asked me about the farm, if I'd "smelled" anything wrong. He got awfully nervous when I asked why but wanted me to "report" to him anything unusual. More unusual than vines killing a random Mundane? Or *in addition* to vines that might kill a Mundane?

It kept coming back to that field, and even though I'd mentioned leshies to my fellow trespassers on our ride home, that didn't make sense. Leshies preferred to tickle sapients with their viney beards, not spear them through the brains...

Through the brains—like I had once seen my nymph friend do with a fox.

Would a nymph go to the Mundane? No, I'd have sensed her presence. Still, it was a lead, and I might as well follow it. I angled away from the Gap and headed to the orchards of the Mercy Sisters and my friend.

I coasted over the neighboring monastic lands and saw a line of brown-robed figures trudging in from the fields. The Silent Brothers must have been cleaning up after the harvest. I'd spent nearly a century with them recovering from my mental and physical injuries from the Great War. They were good to me, but I was very glad not to be pulling the plow any longer. One dropped his basket to wave, then clapped to get the attention of his brethren. I swooped down, passing just above their heads, then returned to my route, flying low over fields heady with fertile, freshly turned dirt.

The sisters' orchards abutted the monastery fields, but as I entered their lands, the sense of healthiness faded. The trees seemed to slump, their branches drooping as if in exhaustion—or grief. Somewhere in my no-longer reliable memory was the nagging feeling that I'd seen this kind of thing before, and my wings pumped harder, propelling me to my friend. I landed at a run, but quickly slowed to a gentle pace when I saw the nymph's tree. One of its thick, sturdy branches had been cut off. The wound had been dressed—by the sisters, most likely. The other branches leaned away from it, so that the painted stub stuck out alone. The entire tree was a sickly yellow, wrong even if it had been a normal tree succumbing to the seasons and not a nymph's tree that should stay eternally green.

I swished my tail, flapped my wings, and hissed softly, calling to my friend in her native language. "What happened?"

The bark shivered and momentarily took the form of a young female, then the nymph burst from her home and threw herself against my shoulder, her sobs half-screams. Around us, the trees and even the grass began to sway and whip back and forth as she told me of strange men coming in the night with an evil-looking device that belched foul-smelling gasses and had whirling teeth.

"They drew a pattern at my roots, and I couldn't move. I couldn't fight them. I couldn't stop them!" She'd curled herself into a tiny corner of her tree and had not moved until she'd heard me call her name.

I didn't bother to ask how long ago. Nymphs understood time, but not in the way most sapients did. Besides, I had a pretty good idea of when. "Can you still feel the branch? Is it still a part of you?"

She'd had a sense of it for a while, just motion, and then pain-violence-dissolving.

She pulled away from me, and her eyes burned with rage. "Let us find them. Let us find them and destroy them. They were human, but two were different. You can find them. You can help me make them pay!"

Humans, but different. Mundanes, probably with a hired mage. "I'll find them," I promised. "I'll get you justice. But you must stay. Heal. Your tree needs you. This orchard needs you."

She turned and gasped, seeing the damage from the outside for the first time. She fled from my side, her feet barely skimming the grass, and threw her arms around the trunk, just above the tar-painted wound. The branches responded to her example and shifted, covering it and her protectively.

I repeated my promise and left her watering the damage with her tears.

The Gap was only a few miles north of the orchard, but the sun had nearly set by the time I arrived. That was just as well, since I had planned to go under cover of night. Real Invisibility was not as absolute as in a D&D game. Even if a Natural 20 meant anything to real magic, a careful observer would notice an odd delay in how the light moved wherever my bulk came between their eyes and whatever was behind me. I was better off with the darkness as additional cover. I intended to pause on our side of the Gap, wait for full night, then slip on the ring as well as activate the protection medallion the sisters had given me. I was not fond of getting shot, and the soldiers on the other side patrolled at night, too.

When I arrived at the Faerie side, however, I found a tent set up, braziers blazing and meats roasting on a spit. The guards were relaxed, feasting and chatting with a clergyman in fine robes. Bishop Aiden, of course. Someone must have sent word ahead.

A guard yelled and pointed in my direction, sparking a tumult of activity. By the time I landed, a platter with a roasted lamb and a shallow bowl of water were awaiting me near the tent where the bishop sat. He himself had tea and bread.

"Are you fasting for me?" I asked.

"For all of us, for the entire situation. My brother and the Duchess are traveling to the White House where the American President lives. Not because of you. The President thinks we need to establish protocols for the Gap. Cardinal Stephen is with him to represent the Faerie, along with a complement of mages."

"But since the Gap is on your brother's land, he gets a say, too. That should be fun." If I knew the Duke, he'd probably demand an annual tariff of cantaloupes, just to be funny. "Even so, some protocols would be a good idea for Faerie." I explained about the tree nymph.

Bishop Aiden nodded. "I went to bless her, but she would not leave the tree. Are you certain it was Mundanes?"

"The device that belches foul gas and has spinning teeth? Mundanes call it a chainsaw. And if she was in fact, bespelled, that means we have a corrupt mage running around. To top that off, I think that's the cause of the trouble on the McTaggert farm."

"I don't understand. Why would a Mundane think mulching a nymph's tree would benefit his field?"

I shrugged. "Why wouldn't they? They still ask if I'm housebroken. They're an ignorant, impulsive species. The more important question is, why would the nymph's branch cause the McTaggert's plants to go into homicidal rages? I mean, I understand why, after what they did to it. It's just defending itself, and without Euphrasia's intelligence to guide it, it's lashing out—literally and figuratively. But how?"

Bishop Aiden stroked his chin as he looked toward the Gap. The dance of magical energies he could not see reflected in his worried eyes. "Perhaps the same way this phenomenon came into being—a fusing of things which were not meant to combine. I fear this will not be the last trouble we see as our worlds reach out to each other. Precautions are not so bad an idea, indeed."

He turned to me. "Is this why you are drawn to return so soon, or are you simply done with your sulk?"

I reared my head back, insulted. "It was not a sulk. It was a renewal, and I feel better now, thank you for asking."

He let a small grin escape his stern expression. "I am glad to hear it. You have removed treasure from your hoard. You know the rules." He pointed to the ring on my pinkie claw.

"It's not a luxury. It's a tool. The Mundanes aren't going to be pleased with my return. I want to be able to move around unnoticed. There's something I need to do—the last wish of a dying man."

"A Mundane? Why would you care?"

Because, even if he had had an ulterior motive, Rip did try to show me kindness, and if it hadn't been for him, I would not have met some Mundanes who respected and liked me in a way no sapient ever had before. And standing there, under a tent, surrounded by Faerie I had known all my life, and lavished with food and drink, I found I missed my new friends and their games and the pizza and even the crowded garage. It hadn't always been fun, but it had been interesting.

When was the last time my life had been truly interesting?

"They're not all bad," I said. "Besides, that's not the point. There's something else going on—something not quite right. I'm not spending the next century wondering what it is, even if you would let me do it from within my treasure trove."

"Then bow your head and receive God's blessing."

He stood and stretched out his palms over me, murmuring in the ancient tongue of the Church. I felt a warmth and a calm settle over me, along with the assurance that I was doing the right thing. Of course, I knew that already. George had made a point of telling me himself, after all.

When he'd finished, a couple of the serving girls approached, shy and giggling, to suggest that they could go through the Gap and talk to the guards...as a distraction, of course. With an indulgent smile and a warning to remember their virtue, Bishop Aiden suggested they take over a couple of platters of food. I agreed. Some things work no matter what species or dimension you come from.

Soon, they were armed with combed hair, clean faces, and huge trays of food. After they marched through the Gap, I gave them a minute, slipped on my ring, and took to the air, crossing the Gap at its highest point.

I'd passed the security perimeter before one of the maidens had finished reassuring the young soldier that "it was just a breeze."

Chapter Thirteen: Ring Around the Damsel

I soared across the long prairie, following the highway to Los Lagos. I had a couple of miles in which to fly and plan. I was still persona non grata; if I wanted to help Cliffman—or avenge him, as it were—I was going to have to do it in secret. Maybe Father would have his chance to play Archibald after all. That, or I convince Bert to let me see all the evidence. I was going to need more information if I was going to help.

Or maybe I didn't. Could I just drop all my suspicions in Bert's lap and be done with it? He's capable and intelligent for a human. It's not like Cliffman was going to come back and haunt me. Even if he did, I knew plenty of priests and mages who could handle one dissatisfied spirit.

When the stretch of plains gave way to suburbs, I angled toward Little Flower Parish. It was quiet; the only people out were safely ensconced in their moving cars, unconcerned about the slight shimmering in the air above them. The ring was working wonderfully. I could easily make it to the parish with plenty of magic left in case I needed to make a secret return flight to Faerie. I could pass on my information, maybe help solve the case if needed, and no one needed to be the wiser.

But then I heard the distant scream.

I really should know better.

I angled west and headed to where the houses started to give way to something Father called trailers. I didn't know what they normally trailed. I'd only seen them stationary. There was a park before the rows of stationary trailers began, a wide area with ill-kept grass, some metal play structures and a parking lot beside a gazebo. In the gazebo, a woman was struggling to break free of a man's grasp. In the parking lot was the convertible that had run over Señora Dona Elena.

Oh, this guy's luck was worse than mine.

I swooped down and landed on his car with a thump and a roar that shook the rickety wooden structure. The car bounced on its shocks and added its plaintive beeps and whoops to the confusion. The man spun around with a curse, letting go of the girl. Wouldn't you know, it was Rae, the hostess from Natura's, and Carlton, the spoiled Mundane "nobleman" who had been harassing her. From the way she took off running while he gaped at me, she was having second thoughts about changing her mind.

I gave him a smile full of teeth. "We should talk about your driving."

When I pin a sapient with The Grin, they usually faint, beg, or run. Carlton did none of the above. He leapt from the bench and started after the girl, yelling, "Get back here, Rae!"

She slowed in her steps.

I had no idea what could make a fleeing girl more important than a threatening dragon, but no way was I letting him have his prize. With a leap and a profound feeling of déjà vu, I put myself between him and Rae.

He had the good sense to stop. He spread his hands wide. "Okay, I get it. You think she needs protecting. I understand that. That must have looked intense back there. Rae, Raebies, I'm sorry."

Behind me, I heard her breathing calm in response to his placating words. Stupid waif. A couple more minutes of his talk, and she'd probably go right back into his arms.

I wasn't ready to let that happen. I took a careful step back, my tail swaying. She had to back up as well in order to avoid getting bumped by me. "Let me tell you what really looked intense. When you ran down an old woman—or tried to. Was that you I heard scream as he drove past, Rae?"

She whimpered an affirmative, then found her voice. "Please, Carling-Darling, we need to tell the police. I'll be with you, I promise. I'll tell them it was my fault, that you thought you'd impress me. You didn't mean to hurt anyone, Carlton, honey."

Nearly every humanoid species had the cliché of a good girl falling for a bad boy, but there was something suspicious about this relationship. Rae tried to circle around me, and I shifted and stepped back again, trying to put more distance between us and Carlton. This time, she stood her ground, so that I almost backed into her.

"No one would have been hurt if it hadn't been for that dragon," Carlton said. "Do you really want me to go to jail for what would have been a harmless prank if it hadn't interfered? Don't you remember what we said to each other when I gave you that necklace?"

"Carlton..."

I steeled myself for some sappy dialogue that would end with her pleading for me to let her go back to the arms of a man who would run down old women because he thought it was funny to scare her. Both Natura and Samwise were wrong about this maiden. I was wasting time I didn't have. Someone was bound to have heard us, maybe even seen me, and called the police. I had to get to Father and tell him what I knew about Rip and the messages. I could tell him about the car and these two as well; maybe if the police got her away from Carlton, she'd be willing to talk.

Then, a funny thing happened. I felt a shimmer of magic emanate from her.

Carlton, meanwhile, continued to wheedle. "We promised. We said if we ever had a misunderstanding, we'd hold your necklace between our hands together and talk it out."

I glanced behind me. Sure enough, she was clutching the charm tightly. Her eyes wouldn't see it, but a glow of magic was traveling along her veins.

"Rae, my treasure, I'm sorry I lost my temper before. I got scared. I forgot our promise. Please, come back to me and let's talk? The dragon won't stop you. He's in enough trouble for killing Mrs. Costa, anyway."

"But you shouldn't have..." Rae started, then fell to sniffling. But she didn't try to move past me. Looked like he underestimated her ability to make good choices. Still, she hadn't let go of that necklace, and for a second-rate charm, it was potent.

I was no wizard to create a counterspell, and I was exposed out there in the park—but I wasn't going to leave the girl alone and vulnerable either. Cursing my fate and blaming St. George, I whipped my tail around Rae's waist and pulled her onto my back. Thus burdened with my screaming, struggling load, I tackled her no-good boyfriend. His cell phone went flying from his pocket. I stepped on it on my way past.

Rae kicked at my ribs and tried to struggle free, but I held her fast and took to the air. I didn't think her screams could get louder, but at least she let go of the charm to grab onto one of my back spikes. Even so, she kept kicking me, and now the charm was pressed between her chest and my back. I could feel the magic tickle along my scales, but dragons are too strong-willed for this kind of magic, and I ranked among the most stubborn of my kind. Her pleas to take her back produced nothing but an irritating itch.

"Keep still. You'll thank me later."

I abandoned my plan to sneak into the parish garage and dropped my cargo off at the rectory. Instead of running to the door, she tried to head back to the park.

I snagged her with my tail. "You're not going anywhere until your head's clear."

She kicked me again. Had I mentioned she was wearing spiked heels? "How could you take me from him? I love him so much it hurts!"

"Lots of things hurt, princess. Love shouldn't be one of them. But this may sting a little."

I hooked her necklace with my claw and yanked it off her neck.

You'd think I'd bitten off a limb. Rae had an impressive variety of screams. She added yet another one as she howled for me to give back her necklace and started to rip at my scales with her fingers.

If I could have eaten the necklace, the magic would have dissolved in my digestive track, but we were going to need it as evidence. Besides, the last time I ate a magical artifact, it took me a century to get over the bellyache. So I looped my tail around her again like a boa constrictor and pinned her arms while holding the necklace as far from her as possible as I tried once more to convince her that her "Prince Charming" was a selfish manipulator who wanted to cheat love.

Into all of this, the porch light finally turned on, and Sister Bernadette opened the door. "What is going on?"

I shoved Rae into her arms. "Take her in the house and don't let her leave. She's under a spell. I'll explain in a minute."

When I was sure the door was shut and Sister Bernadette was obeying me over Rae's objections, I took the charm to the far side of the garden. I looked it over carefully under the motion-activated light. There was a small, red jewel in the center of a gold heart. A twisted irony given the nature of the spell. I buried it among the forget-me-nots. That should help. I headed back to the rectory, surprised I hadn't heard sirens yet.

When I got to the house, Rae had calmed from shrieking and enraged to shaking and confused.

Sister Bernadette had settled her on the couch with a blanket and a cup of tea while Father sat on the coffee table across from her and tried to get a coherent story from her. She just kept shaking her head and saying, "I don't understand."

"I do." I sat down on my haunches with my tail wrapped around me in as non-threatening a pose as I could manage. "The necklace you were wearing—a gift from Carlton?"

She nodded. "He cornered me on the way home one night. He said he wanted to apologize, and he pressed the necklace into my hand. And he said all these sweet words about how smitten he was with me and how he didn't know how to express it, and... I don't know why I believed him, but..."

Calmly, I explained that the necklace had been bespelled. "That jewel that looks like a ruby? It's a magestone—fairly common in my world, and they hold magic. Mages use them to power spells."

"A love spell?" Father asked, aghast.

"Seriously? You think Carlton was thinking of love? No, there are some things you can't magically force, like love. But you can make someone highly susceptible to suggestion. The more contact involved, the stronger the spell."

"That's why he wanted us both to hold the necklace whenever I disagreed with him. How could I have been so stupid?" She set the cup on the floor and buried her face in her hands. Sister Bernadette hugged her.

I said, "Not stupid. Unaware. Let me guess. He pressed this into your hands and said something about how you should try to love him?"

"He said I should believe we belong together. He convinced me to wear the necklace. Just two weeks, he said. It seemed like such a small, reasonable thing."

"And it's been a series of 'small, reasonable things' ever since, hasn't it? Until he decided to run down Dona Elena for fun?"

"What?" Father and Sister gasped.

Rae nodded and sniffled. "I was in the car. He saw her and accelerated. I was terrified."

Father left the room to call the police, while Sister Bernadette passed her some tissue. Her shakes had subsided; the spell was clearing. Now would come anger and regret. Sister seemed to understand that and continued to rub her back and whisper that everything would work out.

"I tried to get him to call the police," Rae continued, "and we held hands and somehow, it seemed all right. I can't believe he made me think everything was all right!"

"He didn't," I told her. "Not completely. You were fighting with him about it again tonight, weren't you?"

"I hadn't seen him all day. My mom took me to Pueblo to go shopping, and I kept thinking about Dona Elena and how wrong we were to keep quiet. My mom kept asking me what was wrong, but I couldn't make myself say anything. I tried to drop some hints, but she didn't get it. I arranged to meet Carlton in the park to try to talk him into going to the police. Only he got mad, and he forgot about the charm. I... What if he'd remembered?"

"Well, don't worry," Father said as he stepped back into the room, buckling on his wristwatch. "We'll take care of it. I just spoke to Captain Beavers. He wants me to go with him to talk to Carlton's father. He thinks the two of us can convince him he needs to do something about his son."

"Why?" his sister demanded. "Beavers should just arrest Carlton."

"For reckless driving, sure. But magical manipulation? That's not illegal in our world. However, Carlton is eighteen, and he needs his daddy's money. If anyone can influence him, it's Mister Quanz."

Speaking of reckless driving... "Hey Father?" I started, then something in me stopped me from telling him my suspicions that Cliffman didn't willingly drive off a mountain.

Father paused at the door, keys in his hand.

"Be careful. I don't trust Beavers."

Maybe it was the way I said it. Maybe recent events had him feeling the same. He nodded. "Quanz is working late at his plant. Maybe I'll just go straight there instead of meeting Beavers first. I'll call you in thirty, forty minutes and let you know what's happened."

Shortly after he left, Rae moved to full-on regret and was sobbing openly. The sounds of her distress drew Teresa out of wherever she'd been hiding. Soon, she was at her side, stroking her hair and shedding a few tears herself.

I was not made for sympathizing. However, there were other ways I could help. I asked Sister Bernadette if I could Xinga Bert. Rae was in full-on regret mode and sobbing softly; Sister waved silently toward the office while continuing to murmur reassurances and ask her if she wanted to call her mom.

In the office, I contacted Bert.

"Vern?" He blinked at my face on his screen, then looked past me to Father's office. He glowered.

Before I could reply to his unasked but implied question, Natura's head appeared on the screen. "Like, wow! Vern, it's so good to see you."

"Natura? What are you doing there?"

"Heat's gotta eat," she said with a laugh and held a bag so I could see. "I always bring Chinese buffet leftovers for the mid shift."

"Vern, should I ask where you're calling from?" he demanded.

Behind them, I saw a wall with framed certificates and pictures of him at various points in his career. Reflected in those, I saw deputies going about their duties. "Yeah... That's not important right now. I need to talk to you about McTaggert's fields. I think I know what's caused the chili peppers to go into a homicidal frenzy." Quickly, I explained about someone attacking my nymph friend's tree.

"Are you saying someone ground up this branch and spread it on that field, like some kind of magical fertilizer?" Bert asked.

"It has to be more than that. The branch should have died, just like with any other tree. Magic must have kept it alive, and if the mage wasn't careful, it could have retained the last impressions of its nymph—fear, rage, and an overpowering need to defend itself—but without her intelligence, it would strike out at any threat."

"All right. That explains the plow driver and the kids who were trespassing—but what about Jace?"

"What if he was beating Teresa?" Natura asked as she unpacked the food. "You said she had fresh bruises. Could it have sensed her distress and wanted to defend her?"

Bert frowned. "Okay, so why didn't it bother the migrant workers when they were out in the fields? And the peppers—we're sure they're not...?" Suspiciously, he eyed the vegetables Natura had set out for him.

"It would not have traveled into the vegetables; don't worry. And the harvest is the culmination of a nymph's purpose. It probably welcomed them. But the plow—a large machine that belched noxious gasses and ripped into it with rotating teeth?"

"Just like the chainsaw," Natura said quietly. "That's so intense. But I don't see McTaggert doing something like this. He's so environmentally conscientious and totally in tune with the universe. That's why I buy from him. He'd never violate a living creature like that."

"He might if he thought it was just an enchanted tree," I said. "From what I've seen of Mundanes, you don't ask questions you don't want answers to, but he was pretty adamant about my not setting foot on his farm. If he didn't know before, he suspected after."

Bert held up a hand to forestall further argument from Natura. "I can get the names of the people who crossed into Faerie."

"They'll have needed the help of a mage," I said. "Bishop Aiden's looking into it, so you'll want to talk to him."

"The Bishop?" Bert asked, then shrugged. "Okay, I'll ask him. And before I have to ask you anything I may regret..."

"There's one more thing," I interrupted. I told him about the message in Cliffman's texts and what I thought it meant. I did not get the response I'd hoped for. Bert didn't see any reason for him to text in code unless the murderer was watching him, in which case, he would not have the chance to text at all, much less in the form of an apology to a dragon. Natura continued to insist that Cliffman would not have gotten drunk in the first place.

"Maybe they forced him to drink?" I suggested, but Bert frowned doubtfully.

"There are plenty of easier ways to kill someone and make it look like an accident. Look, I'll mention the hidden message to CSI. In the meantime, if you are not on your side of the Gap, get there before I or some other authority have to take you back in chains."

Natura promised to fight for me while giving me the "peace sign," and I ended the call. An angry, unsettled feeling in grew my stomach, and I flexed my claws trying to remove the tension in my muscles. What did I expect? Bert was a friend, but he was a Mundane. At least I told him about the message and about Euphrasia, too.

I looked up to the heavens. "I may be the Eighth Day Wonder," I told my Creator, "But thanks to George, whom You sent, I am limited in my wondrous capabilities. And here in the Mundane, I don't even have the glory and authority due my species to fall back on. I've done what I can...unless You have a suggestion?"

I paused then, but nothing happened. Just as well. The last time I'd heard His voice, I was sent after a cursed artifact.

I headed back to the living room. Rae had calmed down, and Sister Bernadette was talking her through the past few days while she took notes. I nodded my approval. Rae was in good hands. I'd resolved to sneak past quietly, retrieve the charm, and get it to Bishop Aiden for safekeeping, when Sister Bernadette said, "What I don't understand is how he got a magic charm in the first place."

"His dad hired a wizard. He was always bragging about it, how the guy was helping them revolutionize the fertilizer industry."

I stopped at the door and turned back to them. "The Quanzes have a wizard? Did Carlton ever mention McTaggert's farm?"

She bit her lip, thinking. "Umm. Yeah, kind of. I mentioned it, when the second death came out in the papers. I asked him if his dad supplied them. He said, 'No worries, Raebies. He's got it taken care of.' And he laughed, and I laughed with him. Ugh. Why did I let him call me 'Rabies'? It's a disease."

"What does 'taken care of' mean?" I asked, dreading her reply. I'd seen enough noir that I thought I knew the answer.

Sister Bernadette caught on fast, too. She dropped her notebook and picked up her phone. "Come on, Richie, pick up. Pick up..."

It went to voice mail.

"Call Bert," I said. "Tell him everything and to meet me at the fertilizer plant. Where is this plant, anyway?"

Rae had already called it up on the map function on her phone. It even showed me a view from above with a line indicating the direction.

I could get used to technology.

As I activated my ring and took to the air, I had two thoughts: one, it was going to be really embarrassing getting escorted out of this universe in chains, and two, I needed to be more careful when I asked God for direction.

Chapter Fourteen: Bad Chemistry, Worse Magic

The plant wasn't far from the parish—past the houses and on the other side of the warehouse district where I'd seen someone breaking and entering the first time we'd gone to the farms. I couldn't help but think if Bert had just deputized me and let me examine the fields, we might not all be in this mess. And for that matter, Father never did much investigative work for me, yet the first time he goes out to confront a criminal—well, talk to the criminal's dad—I had to put myself at risk to make sure he wasn't in danger. Some Archibald.

For being a fertilizer plant, there was nothing plant-like about the building. The large, square, grey factory smelled of ammonia and other noxious chemicals. I couldn't sniff Father out with all that olfactory interference. I just hoped I didn't sneeze at the wrong time.

I found Father's car parked and empty by a covered storage area with foul-smelling bags. They were marked fertilizer. I understood why Natura insisted on organic food. Cliffman had asked me if I'd "smelled" anything suspicious at the McTaggert farm. How ironic I was being forced to endure this stench on his behalf.

Fighting back sneezes, I slunk around looking for Father.

He wasn't in the car, and I didn't see signs of struggle. So far, so good. I headed to the building. No lights shone through any of the outer-facing windows.

I circled the building looking for the entrance he used to get in. I hadn't seen a sign of struggle outside, so he must have been caught after entering, and since I didn't think his desire to play junior detective extended to illegal entry, there had to be an unlocked door somewhere.

I found it, of all places, in a well-lit area just beside the loading bays. He'd even blocked the lock to ensure a hasty retreat. Maybe all those detective stories had rubbed off after all.

I let myself into a large, dark, open area.

I heard voices deep inside. One was praying, his voice straining with effort, as if his prayers were a weapon or a defense.

Father!

I made my quick but stealthy way past bags stacked on pallets and tightly wrapped in plastic. Small vehicles with strange L-shaped handles on their fronts stood guard like eerie sentinels. The smell was even stronger than in the outside storage area. Since my nose was useless for tracking, I followed my ears and my magic-sensing ability. It comforted me that I didn't detect any magic among the pallets of fertilizer. Hopefully, that meant Quanz hadn't violated any other magical trees.

No, the only magic I sensed came from down the hall, in the office area. The words of the St. Michael prayer echoed down the hallway. One of the parishioners at Little Flower had shown me a Mundane picture of St. Michael spearing a dragon. He seemed to think it was proof that I was the enemy of angels and the Church. I wondered what he'd think of his priest praying to Michael the Archangel for aid and having a dragon come to his rescue.

Father sounded determined, stubborn, maybe a little scared, but not in any pain, so I played it smart and slunk down the corridors, keeping below window height and treading carefully. The hall was brightly lit, so anyone stepping out of an office would see me, even with the invisibility charm, but apparently no one was around except Father and his captors. As I neared, I realized they were trying to have a conversation with their captive priest.

Father had switched to the Lord's Prayer: "...and forgive us our trespasses as we forgive those..."

An unfamiliar voice replied, "But that's exactly what we're asking you to do. Forgive us. Just forgive, Father, and forget..."

Father raised his voice. "And lead us not into temptation but deliver us from evil."

"Oh, you don't believe we're evil. You believe –
"

"I believe in one God, the Father Almighty –"

Father's words ended in a grunt as someone backhanded him. So, the unknown voice was probably Carlton's daddy. They must share a similar temperament.

As Father coughed and spat, Quanz howled in frustration. "What's wrong with this thing?"

A man with a Faerie accent replied, "Nothing, my Lord. He's a consecrated man calling on the protection of the Most High. You need patience."

Hey, I'd found the wizard! That must mean "this thing" was a charm, probably like the one Carlton used on Rae. The spoiled apple didn't fall far from the tree, then.

As the wizard started a long explanation about the complexities of using natural magics when combatting a strong Good or Evil influence, I sped up my pace, rounding a corner and rushing past an open doorway. I saw Father's phone, smashed from being thrown against a wall. Guess he got caught trying to collect evidence. I thought about grabbing it, then discarded the idea. I might need all my appendages to free Father. Once again in my time among humans, I found myself wishing for pockets.

Quanz was arguing that the spell wasn't strong enough and that they should try using second charm at the same time. I suppressed a snicker. Stacking spells? Did he think he was playing D&D?

Apparently, this wasn't the first stupid suggestion the Mundane had made, because the wizard sighed with exasperation. "No, I am not going to try. It was trying things your way that got us into this mess in the first place. If you hadn't made me rush the spells with the nymph's tree..."

"Shut up, you fool. The less we have to force him to forget, the better. We don't have time. Beavers is on his way, and he can only turn a blind eye to so much. He helped get rid of the dragon, but he'll draw the line at another human, especially one of our kind. Get the other charm, and let's both try both at the same time."

"It doesn't work that way! Besides, I don't have it. Your son asked to borrow it. Something about a girl."

"He *what?*"

As Lord Spellstacker the Obsessed went into a rant about his errant son, I reached out with my senses. The magic had dimmed, as expected, and neither of the voices came from directly through the door. Most likely, they were stationed near a corner of the room, with no one watching the threshold.

They sounded busy arguing. I chanced a peek in. There was Quanz, dressed in khakis, a suit jacket and a company polo that was as red as his face, screaming at a younger man in a company T-shirt and jeans. I guess wizards didn't rate collars in this universe.

Father sat in a chair, tied hand-and-foot with zip ties. He looked mussed up and was moving his jaw in that way humans do when they get hit in the face hard enough to hurt but not hard enough to break anything. He saw me, and his eyes widened, but he didn't gasp or shout. Instead, he flicked his gaze toward his still-arguing captors and with one hand, held up his thumb and forefinger.

Yes, I knew there were two of them. But Beavers was on his way, and since Father didn't meet him ahead of time, he might come expecting trouble. Besides, knowing Quanz had had something to do with my troubles here in the Mundane had put me in a vengeful mood. If I was going to get kicked out of the Mundane again, it might as well be for a good reason.

I let out a thunderous roar and ran into the room, wings and cheek crests flared, teeth bared.

The men only had time to scream like pixies before I knocked them down. I didn't stop to check the damage but ran for Father and pounced on him hard enough to break the wooden chair. Without waiting for him to extricate himself from the fragments, I yanked him up and pulled him along with me. He limped and staggered as he tried to pull pieces of the chair legs from the bindings on his calves.

"Are you crazy, Vern? You could have broken my ribs!" he complained.

"I knew what I was doing. You'd rather wait until he decided to try something other than a simple charm? Run faster!"

"My phone!" Father started to swerve toward the broken phone, but I shoved him with my snout.

"I got it. Keep going." Behind me, I heard footsteps coming out of the office. As I passed the phone, I swept it up with my tail.

There was a loud report, and something pierced my behind. I howled. Not again!

"Vern!" Father started to slow, but another shot just missed him, and he ducked around the corner. I hurried after him as fast as I could, each step bringing me a fabulous new experience in pain. Another bullet pierced my thigh as I rounded the corner, following Father blindly.

If only one of us had been paying attention, we might not have ended up in the break room.

Father slammed the door behind me, locked it, and got as far from it as he could.

"Vern! Are you okay?" He grabbed some napkins from the counter and tried to staunch the flow of blood.

I yelped as his ministrations just brought more pain. "What do you think? You could have mentioned the gun."

"I did! What do you think this means?" He held up his finger and thumb.

"Two."

"Gun! Everyone knows that's the symbol for gun."

"Every Mundane!" I retorted as he went for more napkins. "Never mind the first aid. We have to get out of here."

As if in agreement, we heard pounding on the door.

"Window," I gasped through gritted teeth. I could not remember hurting this bad since demon-possessed farmers skewered me with pitchforks.

"Plate glass, and they don't open." Father grabbed a chair and flung it, but it barely cracked.

"Move." I extended my claws and swiped with all my considerable strength, scoring four deep lines in the glass. I did it again in the other direction, so I made a nice cross hatch. "Try now."

He swung once, then twice, the glass shattering into spider-web patterns but not quite breaking. Behind us, our pursuers rattled the doorknob. They didn't think to try that first? Then I heard shots and the splintering of the wood around the lock.

We were out of time. I ordered Father onto my back and shoved him on when he didn't move fast enough. I folded my wings over him, backed up, and ran horns first toward the window. It shattered, no match for my 800 pounds of moving bulk. Sharp glass scraped my wings, but my scales protected the rest of me. My leg gave out when I landed, and I toppled, tossing Father off my back. He hit the pavement but rolled to his feet. He ran over to me, but I'd already stood on my own.

A police car barreled up to us, bathing us in the glare of its headlights. Even with my fine eyesight, I could barely make out the door opening. However, there was no mistaking Beavers' voice as he commanded us to stay where we were.

Father put his hands in the air. "Don't shoot!" he called. Guess he didn't want to take any chances.

"And tell them to stop shooting," I added. I jerked my head toward the broken window we'd just crashed through. Quanz and the wizard were there, peering out. Quanz still held his gun, and for a minute, I had the wild hope that Beavers would notice me bleeding, do the right thing, and arrest Quanz.

Beavers looked up. "Are you all right?" he called to the two humans.

Yeah, I should have known it was too much to hope for.

Quanz yelled, "Captain! Thank God you came. That priest and his dragon broke into my factory and attacked us."

Father and I both shouted in protest, but the Captain ordered Father to get on his knees and put his hands behind his head.

I gathered my legs under me for a pounce, but Father stopped me.

"It's all right, Vern. We'll sort this out," he said as he complied with Beavers' instructions.

I grunted in reply. Oh, we were going to sort this out, but I was not going to do it from the zoo. I bowed down, as if acquiescing to Beavers' demand, but the minute he dropped his guard, I intended to launch myself out of there, snagging Father the same way I had Rae. If they wanted to believe I was a wild dragon, then I was ready to accommodate them.

Beavers started out from behind his car, cuffs in one hand, gun in the other. Looks like Father was right about the gun. "I tried to make this easy on you."

"How long have you been in Quanz's pocket?" Father asked.

Even though he was edging toward Father, his attention and gun were focused on me. He laughed in friendly protest. "You've got it wrong, Padre. I'm just trying to keep the town running smooth and happy."

"I'm not happy," I said. I heard cars heading toward us, fast. Had he called for backup? How many people did he have on his side? The bullets were burning in my muscles. I hated it—if there was going to be burning flesh, I should be causing it, not falling victim to it. I wasn't sure I would be able to get very far carrying Father. Did I stick with him or...?

Who was I kidding? I wasn't abandoning Father, even if he was a terrible Archibald.

While I'd been worrying about my butt, Beavers had been running his mouth. "And you weren't making people happy, Vern, were you? Quanz was going to do such wonderful things, combining magic and modern chemistry. He could have solved world hunger once he got the bugs worked out of his formula. But you had to go stick your nose where it didn't belong, and drag your priest friend into it, too. Now, I'm going to cuff the good Padre, and then we're going back inside to discuss this like civilized beings. If you try anything, it won't go well for either of you."

"Andrew," Father said slowly, "listen to me. Quanz has a wizard on his staff. That man with him right now, in fact. He's tried to use a manipulation spell on me. He might have done the same to you."

He wasn't under a spell. I'd have noticed the scent of magic on him. He was siding with the bad guys of his own free will. I could not let us go back into that factory. I was probably going to get shot again. Fewmets.

I pretended to be compliant while I watched for Beavers to lower his weapon so he could cuff Father.

Suddenly, there were lights and sirens as Bert drove his sheriff's vehicle into the parking lot. Following behind were two other cruisers trailed by a van from the TV station. They all pulled up to us, encircling us in light.

"Gunman at the window!" Father called out and two deputies and the camera crew turned their focus to Quanz, who had the good sense to drop his gun and hold up both hands in a show of innocence.

"I was protecting myself. They were breaking and entering. They attacked us!" he shouted, turning to the reporters more than the police.

"Don't listen to him," Father shouted back. "We were trying to escape. They shot at us. They hit Vern."

"Twice!" I added.

"Vern!" Natura dashed out of Bert's car, a first aid kit in her hand. While she knelt to examine me, Bert's deputies made Quanz and the wizard come out to the parking lot, helping them through the window.

Then everyone started talking at once. Father stood and protested our innocence and the brutal treatment by Quanz. Quanz insisted we were trespassing. Natura started yelling about the corporate sector taking the law into its own hands. The reporter called out a question to Quanz while the cameraman inched closer to the window. Beavers was alternating between ineffectively asking everyone to calm down and telling Natura to put on gloves. I, Father, and Natura shouted for him to shut up.

At this point, Bert spoke over his car's loudspeaker. "That's enough. Everybody pipe down. Captain, uncuff Father. He ain't dangerous, and you're outside your jurisdiction, anyway."

As Beavers complied, making noisy excuses and treating the cameras to his most congenial grin, I heard Quanz whisper, "You're a wizard. Do something."

I turned my head around slowly and leered at the wizard. He wilted a little and inched away from his boss. So, he had some brains after all.

His boss, however, was a different story. Again addressing the press and not the police, he said, "Do you see that? Do you see the way that thing is looking at us? I had every right to defend myself. Restrain it before it attacks us all."

"That's not true!" Father yelled. He held up his wrists, still enveloped in zip ties. He pointed to his calf, which still had a piece of chair leg tied to it. "Vern rescued me. He broke me free, kept himself between me and the bullets, and even protected me as we broke through that window in a desperate attempt to escape."

"Which Beavers stopped, by the way," I snarled more than said. Pain was making me crankier than usual, and Natura, while good-intentioned, was not helping much by taping bandages to my scales. "Plus, he handcuffed Father Rich while Quanz was still holding the gun and was going to take us back inside the place we just broke a window to escape from."

"Ridiculous! I only shot at the beast because it attacked us."

"Which is why you shot me in the butt—twice? I'm not a skunk, Quanz. When I attack, I use the other end."

That earned me a couple of snickers, but Quanz was doubling down, insisting that they shouldn't trust Father because he was a priest and they—meaning the press, I suppose—knew all too well that the Church lied to protect what was "theirs"—which, he asserted, included me.

Father's face burned an angry red, but he didn't argue. Instead, he said, "I have proof. I recorded everything."

"He's lying!" Quanz shouted. "He has nothing."

Father gave him a smug and superior grin that was almost dragon-like. I felt my heart warm with pride. "I'm sure you thought that after you smashed my phone. But I was recording with this." He showed everyone his fancy wristwatch.

"I came here to talk to Quanz about his son's behavior. I was expected, so I let myself in through an unlocked door. I heard those two arguing about McTaggert's farms and the magic they'd put on his fields."

Quanz shouted about lies, and Beavers stepped toward Father, saying he needed to confiscate the watch as evidence. Father backed away, holding his hand over his watch protectively while countering that they were in the county now and he'd give his evidence to Bert.

The reporter took that moment to be bold. "What about the McTaggert's farm? What do you mean, magic?"

That was my cue. "There's an orchard in Faerie, not far from the Gap. A nymph has a tree there, and through her magic, the orchard thrives. Quanz or some of his henchmen violated the tree, cut off a major branch which they brought back to the Mundane, and hired this wizard"—I pointed to a now-quaking mass of human misery—"to manipulate the magic it contained."

I faced the wizard more fully. Sweat stained his T-shirt under the armpits, and he could not meet my eyes. I was surprised he was still standing. "I suppose you were looking for the branches' inherent desire to thrive. Instead, you enhanced its instinct to survive at any cost."

"Shut up," Quanz said, though whether to me or his employee, it wasn't clear.

Naturally, I ignored him. "Was it your magic or some kind of weird chemical process that brought that instinct to the fore?"

"I don't know," he whispered.

"Stay quiet, now, sir," Beavers interjected to the wizard, though he gave a glance at Quanz. "You haven't been read your rights, and you don't need to say anything."

"Beavers, go on home. We've got it from here," Bert said. "Juarez, could you show Beavers to his car? And let's go ahead and take everyone back to the station for questioning."

"No!" the wizard shouted, and in a surprisingly agile move, rushed the deputy and grabbed his gun. He pointed it wildly. "I just wanted to help. Quanz said we were going to keep your people from starving. I asked for a seed, and they brought me back the whole branch. I didn't know how they got it. I didn't know about the nymph. I just wanted to help your people."

"Bobby," Quanz soothed, "we can still save the world, but only if you stop talking now and let me handle this."

Deputy Juarez played along. "He's right. No one's being arrested yet. We just want to figure out what's going on. Put the gun down. Nobody needs to get hurt."

He stepped toward "Bobby," halting and holding up his hands when the wizard jerked the gun at him.

"How can you say that? People are already hurt—and worse! The nymph, and those two men in the field, that councilman...and I kept on going. I let this lying pile of iron convince me that we were working toward a greater good, that it would all be worth it in the end."

"Iron?" Quanz asked.

The wizard's quaking had quelled, and his fear of me now turned to anger as he revealed all he felt his boss had tricked him into. He again pointed the gun at Quanz, and his hand was steady. "Yes, iron, you idiot. The one substance in the known universe that destroys magic. That's what you were doing—destroying my magic!"

"Now, Bobby..."

"Bahbianus! My name is Bahbianus. You even ruined that with your shortcuts." His finger tensed on the trigger.

"Bahbianus," I said slowly as with equal care, I turned myself around to face him. "We can heal this—the fields, the tree, Euphrasia—but we need your help. Put the gun down, and I'll take you back to Faerie. We'll start there."

"You don't understand," he whispered, and tears started to fall from his eyes. "It's gone too far for that. All those deaths..."

"They were accidents," the deputy said.

Bahbianus shook his head. "In the field, maybe. But the councilman, that old woman? I should have known. I should have known the kind of man I was working for, why he'd want those charms."

"Shut up!" Quanz yelled and lunged toward Bahbianus.

I leapt, too, knocking Quanz out of the path just as the gun went off.

I knew what a stupid move Bossman was making—and that mine was even stupider. After eight hundred years of protecting sapients, habit was overcoming my sense of self-preservation.

This is your fault George, I thought as the bullet struck me and I hit the pavement hard.

Chapter Fifteen: Confessions and Karma

I was seriously going to have to rethink my instincts in this world.

The bullet shattered a scale and dug itself into my side. As I smacked the ground, howling dragon profanities, Juarez and the other deputies rushed in. They cuffed the wizard and his boss and dragged them to a sheriff's car. Father and Natura rushed to my aid. Beavers tried to look like he was coordinating everyone.

Bert grabbed him by the elbow. "I think you should come in for questioning concerning your involvement in all this. Would you prefer to do it with or without cuffs?"

Beavers pasted on his "always glad to help" smile and let himself into a deputy's car.

Danger over and captured on film, the TV team now rushed in to get close-ups. Of the perps, rather than us hero-types who deserved it. Figured.

Quanz kept insisting I'd ruined his noble mission, but now Bahbianus was confessing everything and making sure his boss got all the mastermind "credit" for every crime.

The villains had been caught. Good had prevailed. I'd even been heroic in front of the Mundane news team. It would have been the perfect time to do something relaxing like pass out, but my body was not interested in indulging my sense of drama. Besides, my pride wasn't going to let me show weakness in front of the Mundanes.

I insisted I could walk. Much as I hurt, it was going to take more than a couple of bullets to keep an immortal creature like me down. Father and I went in Bert's SUV with Natura. I took my time getting in, with Natura clucking over each step.

Tired of the babbling Bahbianus, the reporter had turned our way and started asking me stupid questions like why I'd risk my life for a human.

"You know, maybe if you Mundanes took some time to learn about Faerie dragons instead of making assumptions based on Mundane legends and popular culture, you wouldn't have to ask," I said. Not the most diplomatic answer, but I was feeling cranky. I did have three bullet wounds, and I think I bruised a rib when I landed on Quanz. Plus, my nose still itched from all that fertilizer.

On the way to the sheriff's office, Father played his recording for Bert. He had been about to walk into the middle of a heated argument between Bahbianus and Quanz. It seemed our wizard had been having second thoughts about his ability to resolve the problem in McTaggert's field and had been planning to go to the Faerie Church and confess (in both senses of the word). He believed some of the Church mages would be able to help them.

Quanz was having nothing of it. "Say a word, and I'll have you arrested. One word to Beavers and he'll take care of you the way he took care of that dragon. Or maybe I'll put in an anonymous tip about the circumstances around Councilman Cliffman's tragic death."

Then, we heard a ringing, a curse, and some scuffling. Father paused the recording. "That's when Bernadette called. Don't tell her, though. It's my fault for not silencing the phone. On the bright side, I had the phone in my hands, which is why Quanz thought I was using it to record."

"So, he had something to do with Rip's death!" Natura sounded triumphant.

"That doesn't make sense, though," Bert countered. "He was definitely intoxicated, alone in the car, no fingerprints on the bottles but his, and no sign of coercion."

"None Mundanes would see," I said. "Quanz said something about charms."

"Like the one they used on me?" Father asked. "But Rip was already suspicious that someone was after him, or he wouldn't have been pussyfooting around with an investigation. He would have gone to the police instead of hiring you as a pretense to ask about the farm. But if he was suspicious, why would he take the charm from someone willingly? Bert said there weren't signs of struggle."

A memory flashed across my mind: the pickpocket bumping into Rip, his phone and e-cig flying. The pickpocket had swept them up fast and given them back. We'd thought maybe he'd taken Rip's phone, but now I saw it: the pickpocket pressing them into Rip's hands, speaking quietly and urgently. I hadn't been listening; I'd assumed he was apologizing. What if it wasn't an apology?

"Maybe he didn't know. Where's the stuff Cliff-man had on him when he died?"

"Evidence locker. Why?" Bert asked.

"I need to see it."

"You think something he had was bespelled?" Father asked.

I nodded. At least my neck didn't hurt. "It makes sense. Rae said she couldn't outright tell anyone about the hit-and-run, but she kept trying to give her mother hints. That's what Rip was doing with the texts."

Bert called to have someone cross the Gap and tell Bishop Aiden to fetch a healer for me and bring him to the sheriff's office. He suggested it was safest for me to stay there until everything was figured out, and I had to agree.

I sighed. It had been a long, injurious day. Fortunately for me, Quanz was under the mistaken impression that silver bullets worked best against Faerie, a belief Bahbianus did not correct (a point in his favor). Therefore, while I was in more pain than I wanted to admit, I wasn't in danger of iron poisoning. I'd been through that before, and it's not fun for me or anyone around me.

"You okay?" Father asked.

"I'll be fine." And I would. Already my body was working at healing itself. With a halfway competent healer, I'd be up and moving, albeit slowly, by tomorrow. "I just need food."

"I'm on it!" Natura dialed her phone.

As she ordered some steaks, rare, Father twisted around in his seat to face me.

"You probably saved my life, back there. Thank you."

"That makes four Mundane lives this week. This is turning into a nasty habit," I groused. Then we both laughed.

"Still, I can't believe you just dashed in, even knowing Quanz had a gun."

"I didn't know."

"I did the hand signal." He held up his thumb and finger.

For some reason, that just made us laugh harder.

By the time we got to the office, the local news website was already showing footage of my self-sacrificing rescue, not that Quanz was telling it that way. Oh, no! This was just another incident of dragon attacks, he insisted. The press was playing both sides, asking folks to share their opinions and vote on a Facebook poll about whether I was a menace or not.

With a snarl of outrage, Natura whipped out her phone. "They are totally on my turf now. Don't you worry, Vern."

At least the sheriff's office knew the real story. They greeted us with applause and had already cleared a large area in the conference room where I could flop down in the most comfortable position possible. An EMT came into check my wounds, though he suggested a vet might have been more appropriate. After a couple of minutes enduring his inexpert fumbling with my scales, I was inclined to agree.

Natura offered moral support, and I was only too happy to suggest that scratching behind my cheek crests would help. She did so, in between posts she swore were in my defense. She pillowed my head on her lap and took selfies to post. In the meantime, Bert went to retrieve Cliffman's personal effects from the evidence room.

Natura paused in her texting to muse over Quanz's failed scheme. "Okay, like how would a branch solve world hunger?"

"It wouldn't. Bahbianus was right about Quanz's shortcut. Bahbianus' spells, combined with the violence involved in the theft of the branch, heightened its survival instinct. Without the moral guidance of its nymph, it was primed to react savagely to any threat."

I gave a deputy my statement, leaving out the part about my trespassing in the fields, but including Carlton's nearly running down Señora Costa. That still hadn't been addressed. In fact, looking back, it seemed awfully convenient that Fischer was right there, with a loaded tranquilizer gun.

"You know," I said as the deputy typed up the last few words on his laptop. "You might want to find out why the ICE Fischer-man chose that particular moment to show up, shooting first and asking questions never."

Her social media mission complete for the moment, Natura set her phone down and focused on comforting me. "Do you think he was under a manipulation spell, too? Whoa. Like, how long does it take to cast?"

"The magic is in the gem. It only takes physical contact and a suggestion. From there, it's a battle of wills and skill. If the suggestion is close to something someone might do, anyway, it's easier. In Father's case, Quanz didn't succeed because he didn't want to give him any information, and he was smart enough to call upon God for help. Rae had that charm on all the time, keeping her under a pervasive effect, but Carlton still needed direct physical contact when trying to bend her to his will. As for Fischer, Immigrations Agent and Dragon Hunter, he probably didn't need more than a handshake and a friendly suggestion."

"And Rip's addictive nature probably just needed a good push. Man, that's so tragic."

I finished my statement and the EMT his examination. He offered to try to pull out the bullets himself, but his instruments were stainless steel, which is around 90 percent iron. A few accidental contacts with those tweezers, and I'd be worse off than I was dealing with the gunshots.

He'd just finished bandaging my wounds with clean dressings when Bert appeared, carrying a box, with Father and a half-dozen curious officers in tow. "Sure there's something magic in here?"

"Oh, yeah." I could sense it from across the room. If I could see magic, the box would be glowing dully. As it was, I felt a tickle in my scales.

He set it down in front of me, and I poked through the contents. As I'd suspected, it was coming from the e-cig case. I opened it. Tucked into the mouthpiece of the e-cig was a small gem. Everyone crowded around to look.

"He vaped when he was drinking, didn't he?" Father asked. "So every time he put that in his mouth, he probably triggered a visceral memory of his drinking days."

Natura groaned. "Which someone—possibly Quanz himself—used to reinforce the suggestion that he get wasted and go for a drive. Oh, man. He had this in his mouth all the time. I warned him, it was bad karma."

"I don't know," Bert said, eyeing the e-cig with a frown as he twirled it in his fingers. "That seems pretty far-fetched."

Natura sighed and stood up. "Oh, Bert, open your mind! Do you trust me?"

"Yes..."

She reached out and grabbed his hand in both of hers, the e-cig held between them. "Then tell me, and be totally honest: What are your feelings for me?"

Without hesitation, he replied, "I love you. I've been crazy about you for years, but you're so hard to figure out sometimes that I... Whoa!"

He jerked back, dropping the e-cig, which clattered to the floor. "What the hell?"

"There's nothing hellish about it," I explained. "It's a natural magic, originally designed to..."

But no one was listening. Natura had thrown herself into Bert's arms and was kissing him while everyone around them cheered.

Humans.

Chapter Sixteen: Crazy Cat Lady Comes Through

The healer arrived later that evening and removed the bullets with skilled hands and a pair of thin, wooden tongs. The EMT assisted, commenting that if he'd been thinking about it, he could have done the same thing with chopsticks. I growled to show my lack of appreciation. Even without iron-based instruments, the procedure was, quite literally, a pain in the butt.

Once the operation was complete, the healer insisted that sacred ground would be best for my healing, so I was allowed to stay the night at Little Flower Parish. I slept in the garden between the statues of Mary and St. Francis. The cool air felt good on my wounds, and I preferred the soft grass to the hard cement floor and artificial heater in the garage. I'd also taken the opportunity to dig up the charm from among the forget-me-nots and pass it to the healer to take to Bishop Aiden.

By that time, Rae, feeling stronger, had called her mother and made a statement to the police. I went to sleep sore but with the satisfaction of a job done, if not well, then well enough.

I awoke to the familiar puttering of a car pulling into the parking lot. Fischer stepped out and strode directly to me.

"So," I asked before he could start in, "did you happen to shake the hand of a certain Lord of Fertilizer? I see you're not armed. Does that mean the spell has worn off?"

He scowled. "I didn't need a spell to tell me you are an abomination to this universe."

"Good thing I'm not of this universe. Nice objectivity, by the way. I'll be sure to let your supervisors know."

He snorted. "Don't bother. I'm off this penalty assignment. It seems some Faerie Duke has made a big stink about us trying to deport you. Told the President that if he really meant what he said about embracing the differences between our worlds, we could start with one very different dragon."

I suppressed a groan. Yep. That was Duke Galen all over. I'll bet afterward, he was laughing about it over a beer.

"You wouldn't happen to know if he demanded a tariff paid in cantaloupes?" I asked.

"What are you talking about? Look, any attempt to send you back is cause for an interdimensional incident, but no one said anything about having to welcome you. Understand that while we will not forcibly deport you, I've recommended to the Government of the United States that you are not a Person and have No Legal Rights Thereof."

"Wow," I said. "I can hear the capitals. You have talent."

"Watch yourself, dragon." He turned on his heel and left.

I sighed. I had regained my place in the Mundane—with fewer rights than the migrant workers at McTaggert's farm, but with no one gunning to remove me, either. And, I would guess, that if the Mundanes were to unfairly imprison or harass me, the Duke would retaliate. He had a warped sense of humor, but he did respect me in his own unfathomable way.

I didn't think I'd have as much trouble from the legitimate authorities, anyway. After the incident with Euphrasia the nymph, they would be a little more cautious about how they treated magical beings—and this world was going to need my help.

I could stay. I had a general, if nebulous purpose, but I still had my original problems. I needed income. I needed independence. I needed a lair of my own.

What was my next move?

A hearse pulled up to the church, and Father went out to meet it. He spoke to the driver as two men pulled out a casket and carried it into the building. I heard Dona Elena's name mentioned in hushed, loving tones.

Attending her funeral was as good a next move as any. After all, she died trying to defend me from the powers of ignorance. I hauled myself to my feet and walked to the church, entering through the narthex like any civilized being. I paused at the last row near the baptismal font to get a lay of the land.

The church was quiet, save for the echo of footsteps and the muffled voices of volunteers arranging flowers and photos around the casket under Sister Bernadette's direction. A few people were trickling in, kneeling in the pews.

Teresa glanced up from where she was fixing a photo on a stand. She smiled and gave me a small wave. I nodded back, pleased to see the relaxed angle of her shoulders. Looked like I was in the damsel-saving business. I imagined St. George looking down from heaven, his arm around some other saint—Francis, maybe—pointing and laughing in that big, booming way of his. Mentally, I sneered at the vision.

Someone on earth didn't find it funny, however. Sister Bernadette hastened down the aisle as quickly as she could without projecting alarm to the others.

"Vern!" she hissed. It took a lot of talent, hissing my name. It's really made for growly sounds. She grabbed me by a back spike and all but dragged me to the narthex. "Vern! You can't be here."

"Señora Dona Elena died while fighting for me," I said, keeping my own voice low and reasonable. "I've come to pay her the respect she deserves."

"You can't be in here," she repeated. "People won't understand."

"And as long as I'm confined to the garage, they never will," I retorted. I was too achy and tired to get angry, but I was also not backing down. "I'll stay in the back."

"No, you won't," a man said from behind us. He stepped forward. Behind him, his wife stood, two children holding her hands, one clutching her skirt, and one in a carrier at her feet. They all looked at me with wide eyes—except the baby, who was more interested in its own toes.

"Jerry Costa," the man said to me. He started to hold out his hand, then, embarrassed and unsure, put it back down. "Dona Elena was my great-aunt. Tía was conscious for a few hours before... Um, she told us what happened. She said you saved her life, even after all your fights."

I didn't comment on the irony of her dying after trying to defend me. "She had a stubborn streak and her own kind of fire. It made things interesting."

He grunted in agreement. "She said she might have misjudged you. She called you Señor Vern.

You've no idea what a miracle it is for her to say something like that."

Despite myself, I grinned. "Oh, I might."

He grinned back, but with mournful fondness. "She was sorry for the way she treated you, I think, but I also suspect she enjoyed it. It was the most excitement she'd had in a long time."

At that point, the eldest pulled out of his mother's grip and dashed to his dad. He looked up at me. His eyes were red-rimmed from crying, but he gazed at me with fascination.

"Did Tía Dona Elena really stick her head in your mouth?"

"Yes."

"Can I?"

"No."

He paused to consider, but apparently decided arguing with a dragon at a funeral in front of his parents was not a smart move. "Can you sit with us? I want to tell the kids at school I sat with a dragon."

"Señor Vern won't fit in a pew," Sister Bernadette protested weakly.

The boy stepped closer to me and leaned in a little, looking up at Sister Bernadette with pleading eyes. I gave her a humble gaze of my own, though I really wanted to smirk. This kid had skill. I could almost feel Sister's resolve wilt.

"...but what if he walked down the aisle with you and sat to the side?" she offered.

The boy and I both looked at his father. Jerry nodded.

Jerry picked up his daughter, and together, he and his wife led the way with their children. I followed with the boy, who whispered his name to me. Other mourners had filed in while we'd been talking, and they all watched us with varying degrees of wonder and aghast. No one broke the respectful silence of the procession with protests, however. At the front of the church, where the choir usually sat, a woman in dark but not mourning clothes was snapping photos. Figured a reporter would cover the funeral. I wondered how she'd play this story, then ignored her in favor of caring for the little boy sniffling at my side.

As we walked down the aisle, Jerry Junior put his hand on my flank. At the casket, I let him climb onto my shoulder so he could see his aunt. Even in the peace of death, she looked like she was ready to take on the world, beating it with her walker and sticking her head down its throat in search of what she knew had to be there. I was going to miss her.

"Do dragons cry?" he asked.

"No, but they can feel sad," I told him.

From the pew, his little sister called out, "Kitty!"

Wouldn't you know, there was Sacha, traipsing over from a side door, three kittens trailing behind her.

A week later, I found myself in the offices of Scott Youngman, Esq., with the sheriff at my right, a restauranteur/social justice warrior at my left, and a disinterested secretary at her desk, typing on her computer as if we weren't an unusual sight at all. I wondered if Youngman paid her a bonus for maintaining such a cool demeanor.

There were two TV screens in the reception area. One was playing a rotating news feed that moved across major headlines. The other played the recording of major network arguing about me.

Anyone reading the *Los Lagos Gazette* the morning after Señora Costa's funeral, hoping to enjoy a scathing article about the first woman dead from dragon attack, had the shock of their lives to see the dragon comforting one of Dona Elena's great-grandnephews. Jerry Junior and I got our photo in the paper while Jerry Senior explained the actual story. That, combined with a video of my taking a bullet to save someone who had already shot me himself, had propelled my story to the national news. I'd had one interview, with Bishop Aiden at my side and Fr. Rich surreptitiously stepping on my tail to make sure I behaved myself.

Now, two women and a man were arguing about the validity of my heroism—one kept saying "Fake News" like it was a cantrip. When they took calls from the viewership, things ran largely in my favor. Natura's social media response team was a force to be reckoned with. At the end of the discussion, the TV people were still skeptical, and the world divided but at least not in favor of sticking me back into a zoo.

The debate ended, to be replaced with other recorded segments concerning me. For my amusement, I assumed. In the national scope, I was already old news, overshadowed by a unicorn who was going to go on a world tour of the Mundane to promote chastity. Apparently, that was more a newsworthy controversy than whether a live dragon should roam free.

I wasn't complaining. I had won the round, conditionally, in the local arena. I was no longer confined to the parish, and while some people crossed the street at the sight of me, others crossed over to meet me and ask questions. Yes, even whether I was housebroken, but at this point, I was willing to take that in good humor.

Speaking of amusement, a new recording played, and Captain Beavers, former Chief of Police of Los Lagos, hurried out of the police station, his hand up to forestall reporters' questions and to block his face from the camera. He'd had to resign as chief of police under suspicion of "irregular activities in the exercise of his authority." The city council asked Bert to take over for the time being until they found a new chief. Hopefully, they would find someone who wouldn't try to run a smooth operation by brushing problems under the rug.

"And they'd better find someone soon," Bert grumbled as he watched himself shake hands with the mayor. "My plan was to have one more, preferably relaxing, term, then retire. Now, I have twice the work and more."

Natura leaned behind me to pat his leg. "You're still young and vital. You can handle it. Besides, now that we're an item, you can come to my place after work and take off the uniform, and I can help you relax."

That drew a sidelong look from the secretary.

Bert sighed loudly, "For the last time, I am not letting you stick needles in my back!"

"As you wish," she'd soothed, but I had had the feeling the argument wasn't over.

Just as the scene cut to Bert standing at a podium to make his speech about agreeing to accept the position of interim Police Chief, the secretary looked up from her desk. "Mr. Youngman will see you now."

She pressed a button, and the large mahogany door bearing Youngman's name clicked open. Then she went back to her typing, seemingly oblivious to the novelty of a dragon was walking into her boss's office.

Youngman's office was large and expensively decorated...and the coffee table and chairs had been pushed to a corner to give me plenty of room to stretch out. Nice touch.

Youngman was closing his laptop. He smiled and stood as we entered. "Vern! Natura. Sheriff. Or should I say, Police Chief? So glad you could make it. You had an uneventful time getting here? Good, good."

As he spoke pleasantries, he undid his tie and took off his button-down, revealing a white muscle shirt underneath. "I hope you don't mind," he said as he slipped off his shoes. "I just got out of a high-level meeting, and as soon as we're done, I need to head straight to Colorado Springs to catch a flight to DC to talk to some senators before the hearing concerning the accident that caused the Gap. I have no time for a stretch, and you've been very understanding about my multitasking. As Natura says, it's nice to have such a chill client."

"It's true," Natura added. "We could learn so much from you about inner peace."

Inner peace? More like exterior exhaustion from trying to figure out the Mundane race. I decided not to comment on that.

I shrugged and scooted over so he could roll out his mat. George and I had had many conversations while he did swordsmanship routines. Why should this be any different?

Natura started to slip off her shoes, but Bert stopped her with a hand on his shoulder. She rolled her eyes at him, but went docilely enough to sit beside him on the couch, giving me some semblance of privacy with my attorney, who promptly took a seat on the floor and started to shake out his legs and arms.

"Why am I here?" I asked.

He set some papers in front of me, then reached for his toes. "It seems Señora Dona Elena Costa had a change of heart concerning you, and she altered her will just before she died to reflect that. She felt you should have a place of your own, so she's left you one of her warehouses."

"A warehouse?" My mind flashed back to the huge, squat structure I'd seen some kid break into. That was less than a month ago, and I'd been wondering if I could get a job protecting it. Now I owned one?

"It's one of three warehouses her late husband owned," my bendy lawyer said. I marveled at how clear his words were, considering his nose was pressed against his knees. That's enunciation. "The other two, she left to Jerry Costa along with the pawn shops. It's not the best kept of the three, and it's been neglected for the past six years, but it's the largest. Dona Elena said you should have room to grow."

"Grow? What am I, koi? Can I sell it instead?" I wondered how long I could live on the profits.

He crossed one leg over the other, braced an elbow against his knee and twisted. With his free hand, he flipped to a page marked with a pink Post-It. "I'm afraid not. The government is willing to let you keep the property, as long as you make it your permanent residence. You cannot sell it nor give it to anyone as long as you wish to remain on this side of the Gap. There will be some expenses associated with ownership, of course, but Mister Costa said he'd help you with them in exchange for anything left of value inside the warehouse."

Natura gave a happy squeal. "Vern! You have your own digs!"

"That'll make Father happy," Bert said. "Now he won't have to figure out how to explain to Sister Bernadette about you 'going' in the garden."

Natura smacked him.

Soon, I was signing papers, a copy of which was presented to me along with a binder about the rules I'd have to follow. The cover had a dragon posed in front of SOLD sign and the title, "Lair Ownership for Dragons in the Mundane."

"My intern compiled it for you. I thought you might appreciate the whimsy," Yogaman said as he straightened his tie, the image of a high-powered lawyer once more. "Be sure to pay attention to the section on taxes."

Great. Now I had to pay annual tribute? George was probably bent double laughing.

The next week found me in my new digs, as Natura called it. Calling this dump "digs" was an insult to dwarves, but at least it was mine.

I was once again among by friends, with dice, pizza, and a fifth-level wizard who was still irate that I'd stolen his ring of invisibility.

"Why don't you roll to see if you can get it back?" I asked Samwise.

With a scowl that was only half in character, he said, "*Accio* ring!" and rolled. "Ha! Eighteen with bonuses."

"The ring floats from Pegjanu's pocket and into your hand," Ray intoned.

At this point, I pulled out my actual ring of invisibility and placed it into his open palm. "It's got about two hours of spelltime left."

"I can rechar— Wait, what? This is real?"

Everyone leapt from their seats to crowd around him, making appreciative sounds.

"Well, you did get us onto McTaggert's farm," I said.

"Lucky dog!" Owen said. "Just don't go using it to impress cheerleaders."

Samwise snorted. "With my luck, I'd attract Nazgul instead. Nah, I'm going to be more patient. Work on myself so when the right girl comes around, I'll be ready."

"'Work on yourself'?" Ray asked. "Can you sound more defeated?"

"Stop it! Samwise is wise," Linda crooned.

"What's this about McTaggert's farm?" Father asked. Despite his earlier protests about not having time, he had become a regular. Sister Bernadette insisted it was the pizza, and I couldn't disagree.

Quickly, we explained about our midnight foray into the fields.

Father sighed and shook his head. "I'm so glad you didn't say anything to me then. But really, what were you thinking? What if someone had been hurt or killed?"

"With Vern there? It was the greatest night of my life," Samwise said. Apparently, he'd already forgotten being nauseous and nearly squeezed to death by angry plants. Or maybe he did remember. Humans were like that.

Instead of arguing, I said, "You could even say it was de-vine."

Father groaned, but I persisted. "Truly. Consider the irony of the plants gaining consciousness on the one farm that 'got Woke.'"

"Vern!"

"Sorry, should I leaf off the plant puns?"

He glared. "Keep it up and I'm going to invest in a Taser."

"Oh? Would you charge it at the power plant?" Owen chimed in, and Father turned his angry look on him.

"Sorry, Father," he said. "You're right. It was dangerous and not a laughing matter."

Mollified, Father said, "It's okay. At least we got everything figured out."

"Yes," I said, "*en viñas vertias*."

I heard the familiar purr of a Lamborghini, so I interrupted what would have been a bountiful pun fest and prepped everyone so that when Youngman came in, we all chanted, "Hot Yogaman!"

He squinted as if in pain, but was smiling, nonetheless. "I'm not going to live that down, am I?"

"Guess you'll have to be more flexible," Owen retorted and had chips tossed at him.

Youngman again treated us to his pained smile. "Well, I'm just here on my way to court to get you to sign the last of the papers." This time, he'd brought his own ink bottle.

Once I'd put my signature on the papers—which, considering I wasn't recognized as a legal person, made me wonder about the legality of it all—he handed my copy to me and put the rest in his briefcase. "That's everything, then. Enjoy your new home."

He left through the warehouse's garage door—the only one that worked at the moment—and we heard his car purr out of sight. He was probably eager to get out of this neighborhood. Not that I blamed him. The first night, I had to scare off three wild dogs, one bum, and one youth who threw his crowbar at me before retreating. Not to mention the rats, but I, Sacha, and the kittens had those under control.

I considered it a testimony to their courage and regard for me that my friends had braved the neighborhood for a "housewarming" of pizza and D&D.

"She just left you this place?" Samwise asked. "Why?"

"Apparently, she told Youngman I needed 'room to grow.'"

"What are you, koi?"

"That's what I said!"

Owen chuckled. "So, you have the land, the building, and all this stuff?"

I nodded. Dona Elena's late husband had apparently made his living doing something called eBay, which seemed to involve buying worthless dreck at garage sales and after-holiday specials, then trying to sell it online at marked-up prices. Judging from the disrepair of the warehouse and the stacks upon stacks of boxes, he was not very good at it. Jerry Costa and his wife, who had inherited the house along with the other warehouses and pawn shops, were moving from Chicago to start their life anew. They'd dropped by to assess what I had, and after looking into a half-dozen boxes, apologized and offered to help me however they could. I didn't find that a good sign.

Ray said, "No offence, but it's a dump. Can you sell it? Get someplace nicer?"

"Nope. Not until I'm ready to return to Faerie permanently."

"Bummer. What are you going to do with all of it?" Linda asked.

I shrugged. I had found several boxes crammed with tiny plush toys and plastic jewelry. We stuffed them into a side closet, the bottom half of which Father blocked with a piece of plywood. I couldn't stretch out much, but I could sleep on my back.

"I'll figure it out as I go along. Apparently, there's not much of value, but treasure's treasure."

"Even the donut?" Samwise asked.

The donut had been a gift from the Sheriff's office—a large round cushion signed by everyone in the department. I was supposed to sit on it for some reason, but since I didn't sit the way humans did, it felt weird and had thus become an enclosed resting spot for the kittens.

"Even the donut," I said. "I'm learning to appreciate the oddities of my new world."

"Speaking of oddities," Ray cut in and took on his dungeon master's voice. "You find yourself transported into a curio shop. Oddities both occult and mechanical crowd the shelves. In the back corner at a counter sits a wizened gnome..."

Humans were made in God's image.

Dragons, on the other hand, were made of God's Imagination, the eighth day creation, limited in number but unending in days. God gifted us to the Faerie world so no one would forget His great power and the wonder of His imagination. We commanded the respect of empyrie from Urkuk, the Harbinger of Hiccups, to Zeus himself. Elves described our virtues in poetry that took days to recite. Dwarves honored us by creating expansive cave lairs. And humans? Well, Image often clashed with Imagination. Nonetheless, even humans acknowledged our majesty.

I am a dragon, and once I was one of the greatest of my kind.

I'm not telling you this to brag. I'm telling you this so you can appreciate the ineffability of God's plans that I, the Great Imagining, should humble myself to live in a dump in a bad part of a Mundane town with rats to eat, cats for companions, and no vision of prosperity in sight.

And yet, despite all that, as I looked around the card table at the Mundanes who had come for no other reason than to play with me, I found I was happy.

Acknowledgements

This book has a very long history with more emotional ups and downs than Vern went through. Buy me a coffee if you want the whole story, but suffice to say, this book would not be here if not for some wonderful people.

First, my husband Rob, for always believing in me, my stories, and Vern.

Next, Jane Lebak, who was always there with inspiration and to back up my instincts, even when I fought them myself.

Matt Souders was in the original crit group where I workshopped this story (and then the disaster of the book it first morphed into) before we moved to another crit group. His encouragement got me through some discouraging times. Thanks for commiserating and for not letting me give up on the story.

Last, but by no means least, the Catholic Writers Guild SFF Crit Group. I joined this group when I was in a dark place not only in my writing but in my life. They listened to my complaints, gave me virtual shoulders to cry on, and prayed, prayed, prayed! For the book, they led me though the mess of a novel I thought would be the origin story, always giving sound advice while letting me stay true to the characters and the world. When I decided it was simply the wrong book, they were glad to do it all over again with the one you now hold in your hands. Plus, they've put up with me when I've been cranky in crits or too silly or had to drop out for a bit for life reasons. Anyone who says you can't form deep friendships online has not been part of a group like this.

Thanks for Reading

from Vern

This book has been a long time coming. I am an immortal creature, so you'd think the wait would not have bothered me, but this book is about me, after all. Since eating my own author would have been counterproductive, I had to resort to nagging. And I did, trust me. I was in her head constantly until this book got written.

Now that I have firm residence there, I don't intend to let up. I can be a creature of habit if need be. Stay tuned for more great adventures. In the meantime, sign up for Karina's newsletter at eepurl.com/dc-8M or follow me on Facebook at https://www.facebook.com/DragonEyePI.

Sister Grace and I don't meet for a couple of years, book-time, but we'll get to her. I am not letting the author forget her. Sister Grace is more patient than me about it.

Made in the USA
Columbia, SC
30 October 2022